The Shockoe Slip Gang
A Mystery

Patricia Cecil Hass
Illustrations by Laura Corson

WINDSONG PRESS

This is a work of fiction. Names, characters, places, and incidents either are the product of the author's imagination or are used fictitiously. Any resemblance to actual persons, living or dead, events, or locales is entirely coincidental.

Copyright © 2019 by Patricia Cecil Hass
Illustrations copyright © 2019 by Laura Corson

All rights reserved. No part of this book may be reproduced or used in any manner without written permission of the copyright owner except for the use of quotations in a book review. For more information, address: hassoffice@verizon.net.

Library of Congress Control Number:2019914635

First edition October 2019

Cover and interior design by Kristin Lohr

ISBN 978-0-578-55877-6 (hardcover)
ISBN 978-0-578-58215-3 (paperback)
ISBN 978-0-578-58211-5 (ebook)

For my husband, Anthony,
with my gratitude and love.

When I was little and lived in Richmond, birds sang and trees bloomed, and children rode their bicycles everywhere. Richmond was a perfect city for riding bicycles, especially in the summer. Green branches hung over the lovely streets, and there were just the right size cobbled alleys, freely wandering dogs and cats, and cool back gardens to explore.

But danger roamed in Richmond, too, and one hot, pulsing summer night, riding along the moon-drenched, silver-dappled avenues, I came to his dark street, and found him.

– Author's note

CHAPTER ONE

Andrew walked out on the back porch, holding a tall glass of ice cream in one hand and pouring ginger ale in it with the other. He looked out across the back yard, shimmering green in the afternoon sun.

"Sally?" He called.

"Here." Her voice came from a clump of trees in a corner of the garden's brick wall.

He picked his way across the grass, thick and bouncy from the July heat, and edged under the tree branches. "What're you doing?"

"Reading." She looked down at him. "A book Mom gave me. It's good, about this guy who's got a gang and rides around on a horse. He wears a mask so nobody knows who he is, but when he goes away he always leaves his mark, a big Z. His name's Zorro."

"Is that all he does?"

"No. He helps people."

Andrew handed her his glass and swung himself up on the wall. "Too bad he's not here. I could use some help with my yard work."

Sally sucked white foam from Andrew's drink and tried to picture a masked man galloping around their city with a band of followers behind him, their horses prancing and rearing. She pulled one knee up under her chin and picked absently at a scab. "Nobody like that would ever come to Richmond. It's too normal here."

Andrew grinned. "We could try to make it weird." He stretched out on his back on the ivy-covered wall, knowing just how to do it without falling off. It was cool under the trees and sparrows cheeped in the branches over their heads. They could hear the sound of cars swishing by on the street in front of their house and see their orange cat, Peaches, walking toward them across the grass.

A door slammed inside the house, and they heard Jane, their little sister, calling their names. The terrace door burst open and she nearly fell onto the flagstones, but she caught herself and ran onto the grass, her curly brown hair flying around her face. "I'm getting to wear eye-glasses!" She shouted, sounding pleased.

Andrew jumped down from the wall and picked her up, throwing her over his shoulder and racing up and down the lawn. "She can see! She can see!" he shouted, as Jane screamed with delight. He dumped Jane on the grass and sprawled beside her, and Sally sat up.

"So when are you getting them?" she said.

"I don't know, but I can stay with my grade next year." Jane petted Peaches, who had climbed onto her lap.

"That's good," Andrew said, remembering how hard last year had been for Jane, for all of them. It wasn't only

the glasses. She had had trouble concentrating too, after their Dad died. That had been a year ago, on a hot day like this, when a drunk driver swerved into the wrong lane and slammed into Dad's car. He had been heading home from work early, except that he never made it. Andrew felt his eyes watering at the memory, but Jane didn't seem to notice and Sally, who usually noticed everything, was still on the wall.

Jane squinted up at her. "I have to go to summer school over again though."

"You might not mind it this time," Sally said. "With glasses you can see the work."

"But she won't be able to help me." Andrew stood up. July and August were his busiest months, when his lawn business expanded into house and pet sitting. He looked at Jane. "Where's Mom?"

"She went back to the office." Their mother worked at the city's fine arts museum, and she had just been assigned to organize a new exhibit of antique American toys. It was a big promotion, and it had come in the nick of time for their family's finances. They'd been on a tight budget since Dad died, with not enough money for any extras like guitar lessons or travel. Even class trips were a luxury. Mac — their part-time housekeeper — was still with them, but only because she'd agreed to work in exchange for room and board while she went to the business college downtown.

Jane pushed Peaches away and squatted on her

heels. "Mom works too much," she said. "I liked it better before she got promoted."

"You know why she has to work so much," Sally said, her voice rising. "Besides, this whole exhibit was her idea. She wants to make sure it's good."

"I know," Jane nodded glumly. She stood up. "Anyway, she said if you're going swimming to take me."

Andrew grunted. "Okay. But I have to feed Mr. Kelso's pigeons on the way."

"I'm coming too." Sally put her book in a tin box in the ivy and dropped to the ground. They walked across the grass, blinking in the sunlight, into the dimness of the cool, high-ceilinged house.

They could hear Mac on the second floor, vacuuming and singing at the same time. Mac was tall and bony, with yellow hair and pale skin. She often sang really loud while she worked, which she said helped whatever was bothering her.

"She sounds awful today," Sally said.

"It's her feet." Andrew picked his bathing suit off a hook in the back hall. "She sounds off key like that when they hurt."

"So?"

"So, let's get out of the house before she finds stuff for us to do," Andrew said.

Sally and Jane grabbed their suits and towels and slid through the side door behind him. They wheeled their bikes along the cool walk beside the house and bumped down two steps to the sidewalk in front.

Their house stood on a tree-lined avenue divided in the middle by a wide grass plot edged with green maple trees. Traffic was light in mid-afternoon, and the city hummed gently around them, making Sally's thoughts drift to Zorro and his gang. It would be so cool to see guys like that, riding right up to her, their horses snorting and pawing the ground.

"Sally?" Andrew called. He and Jane were already halfway up the block, looking back to see where she was. Andrew was eleven — a year younger than Sally — but two inches taller and fifteen pounds heavier, and he could ride very fast.

"Coming!" She started moving, pedaling hard along the next two blocks, before they turned onto a boulevard lined with more houses, a history museum, and the big Fine Arts Museum where their mother worked. Andrew pulled up in front of a row of houses across from the museum and set his kickstand, looking at Jane.

"If you come with me it'll save time. You can change the water."

Sally waited with their bikes, leaning on her handlebars. A month before school ended she'd hurt her leg playing Lacrosse, which had put her on crutches for six weeks. She still felt out of shape, and now sweat trickled down her arms and legs as she moved into the shade of a persimmon tree, pushing back her helmet. Absentmindedly she looked around, and then her eyes stopped. Across the street in front of the museum a man sat quietly idling his motorcycle. He was wearing a headlamp and a heavy black canvas jacket. A crowbar was sticking out of one of his pockets.

"In ninety degree heat in the middle of the day?" She said aloud.

He couldn't have heard her, but he looked in her direction, and she couldn't help staring back at him.

"Done." Andrew's voice came from behind her. "Let's go."

"Wait." Sally's mouth barely moved. "Don't look, but there's a weird guy over there."

Andrew eased onto his bike. Then he leaned over, pretending to tie his shoelace. "He must be melting. And what's with the headlamp?"

"He's a terrorist." Jane had come up behind them. She sounded scared.

"Don't be silly, of course he's not." Sally said.

"Maybe he's waiting for dark, to rob a store or something," Andrew said. "Let's check him out."

They walked their bikes along the sidewalk, pretending to be heading toward the museum's landscaped parking area. They could see the man on the motorcycle had taken off his headlamp and put on his helmet. He looked around quickly, then saw them and stopped, staring at Sally again. His look made her shudder, as though he was sending some evil spell in her direction. She stepped back quickly, moving behind one

of the parked cars, and when she looked out again the man had dropped his gaze and was rolling his motorcycle slowly forward, gently revving his motor. Suddenly he accelerated and shot off along the Boulevard, veering around the next corner until he was out of sight.

Sally pulled on her bike helmet. "What a creep," she said shakily.

"He knew we were watching him," Jane said, sounding worried.

"Maybe," Andrew said. "Anyway, he's gone. Come on, let's go swimming."

Four blocks west they crossed the downtown expressway and turned into a quiet lane lined with trees. At the end, a high chain-link fence surrounded an old stone quarry, now filled with water, amber-colored and dappled with shade. Children floated in inner tubes in a roped-off area, and some adults were swimming slow, circular laps around the edge.

Andrew and Jane propped their bikes at a stand inside the gates, but Sally moved hers closer to the bathhouse when she saw a lady waving at Andrew. He would drop anything for a new customer, but Sally and Jane were too hot to wait. They changed into their bathing suits, rushing out and flinging themselves off the stone dock, heading for the raft. The water felt cool and wonderful, and Sally rolled over and lazed on her back, staring at the sky through the trees, thinking how good she felt in the summer.

Jane had climbed up the raft's ladder and sat down, scowling. "Nobody I know's going to be at summer school," she said. "Everybody's either away or doing something else. Like earning money, the way Mom needs us to."

Sally climbed up beside her and reached over to rub her sister's small, bony shoulder. She knew Jane never used to worry like this before Dad died, but now it seemed like she was always scared of something. "It'll be okay," Sally said. "You can still earn money after you finish summer school. And don't forget your new glasses – they'll look great, like you're a brain," she teased.

Andrew had reached the ladder and hung on, his fingers looking brown. "That person in the parking lot wants her cat and dog fed, and the dog walked," he interrupted. "And her yard done once a week for the rest of the summer." He looked at Sally. "I could do a lot more if you'd help, now your leg's okay."

Sally rolled over. "I have to do my reading list."

"You can read at night," Andrew said. He heaved himself up onto the raft. "You could help in the day, instead of lying around."

"I'm not lying around. I just don't want to cut grass." But even as she said it, she knew Andrew would have trouble finding someone else. Most kids had summer jobs or were away at camp or in some kind of program. She was practically the only person she knew who wasn't doing anything, and now that her leg was healed she ought to be earning money too.

"You always wanted to do stuff before," Jane said. She was blinking hard, a sign she was upset. "You've been acting weird all summer. Why'd you get so lazy? Mom said we all need to help each other."

"I know what Mom said. Just back off, will you?" Sally slid off the float into the water and started doing kicks on her back, already sorry for the way she'd sounded. Was she really lazy? She didn't think so, but she had to admit Andrew was right – she could easily do the work he needed. The trouble was that she liked doing nothing. It felt more like her old life, the one when she was a kid, not the responsible oldest daughter she'd had to become after Dad died. All she really wanted was to bury herself in the summer's heat, sweet-smelling grass, and deep greens and blues, and keep those inside her head to help her feel safe and whole, before the cold of fall and winter returned and the emptiness without Dad came back to live inside her.

    Still she felt guilty, and she couldn't shake off a feeling of doubt as they left the quarry and got on their bikes. Lost in thought on the way home, she looked up as they were passing the museum and Mr. Kelso's house, and she felt a quick shiver, remembering the guy on the motorcycle. She slowed and looked around, hoping he was really gone. What if he wasn't, she thought. What if he's watching us, from somewhere we can't see? She shook her head, knowing she was being silly, but then, not understanding why she couldn't shake her uneasy feeling, she kept looking behind them all the way home.

CHAPTER TWO

"Zorro was an old TV series," their mother said at dinner. "I used to watch reruns when I was growing up, and I loved it."

"You're not going away again, are you?" Jane said suddenly from her seat at the middle of the table. "I want you to stay home."

"Let's get these conversations together." Mrs. Corbett smiled at her daughter. "No, I won't have to travel again. We have all the toys – the last ones arrived today, including a miniature wooden cannon."

Andrew perked up. "Can you set it off?"

His mother laughed. "It's over 200 years old. Not strong enough to be fired. It's belonged to the same family for generations and they're very attached to it, so I wouldn't want it to blow up."

Sally speared more tomato slices onto her plate. "It'll be fun to see these new ones."

"Yes, but I love all the toys," Mom said. "And having so many of them here is really exciting. It could give our museum a big boost."

Outside the dining room windows the cicadas were buzzing, and Andrew helped himself to a third ear of corn. He slathered it with butter, which dripped onto his third biscuit.

"I got a new customer today," he said. "When we were at the quarry. That makes as many clients as I can handle. Dad would...," he stopped.

"Dad would what?" his mother asked gently.

Andrew put down his piece of corn and stared at it before he answered. "I guess I'm hoping he'd be proud I have so many." Dad had been an investment advisor, with lots of clients of his own. "I should bring in almost a thousand dollars this summer."

Mom smiled wistfully, watching Andrew blow on his ear of corn before taking a bite. "Yes, he would be proud of you. I'm proud of you too. And we do need the money."

Sally batted her biscuit away from the tomato slices on her plate so it wouldn't get soggy. She sighed. Andrew could be bossy, but he was an okay brother, and he needed her. *I better tell him I'll help him*, she thought, as Mac walked in from the kitchen, bearing a steaming dessert. She looked belligerently at Mrs. Corbett and sat down. "You forgot the ice cream, so I made bread pudding."

"That's wonderful," their mother said. "You know we couldn't survive without you. Or your bread pudding."

"I hate bread pudding." Jane pushed back her chair.

"Don't leave," Mom said. "We have to finish filling out those school forms."

Andrew could tell Jane was going to start an argument, and he jumped up. "I've got to feed some dogs. I'll grab a popsicle in the kitchen."

Sally half got up too, looking at her mother, who nodded.

"Listen," Sally said to Andrew as she followed him out. "I'll help you. But if I don't like it, you'll find another person, okay?"

He nodded, looking pleased. "Yeah, sure. Thanks. Meet me out front."

It was still light when they swung onto their bikes and started down the grass-plot. Cicadas buzzed in the ivy that climbed on the houses, and the warm air smelled sweet and soft. The avenue stretched ahead of them to Meadow Street, misty in the evening glow. They pedaled three blocks, not talking, until Andrew cut right on a side street into a paved alley.

Mulberry trees hung over the back garden walls and dogs barked as they passed. Halfway down the alley Andrew coasted to a stop beside a fence. A big brown and white collie stood whining and wagging his tail.

"That's Bruce," Andrew said. "He always worries when I'm late."

He pulled a wadded piece of paper out of his pocket and unfolded it. "All the dogs I've got on this block are friendly, so we can split up to feed them. The food's in that garage."

They worked quickly, mixing the food with water, taking the bowls to Bruce, to a Springer Spaniel, two labs and a bouncy Dachshund named Jerry. Afterwards they took the dogs to a little fenced triangular park, where they sat on the grass watching the streetlights come on. Swallows flew over their heads as it slowly grew dark, children played hopscotch on the sidewalk across the street, and a bat swooped in the silence of the dusk. Sally rubbed Bruce's head, wishing they could linger in the park until the sky turned midnight blue.

"Look at all these houses," Andrew said, half to himself. "Yards, dogs, cats. What a profit situation. If we had more people we could do these gardens too."

"Andrew, stop," Sally said. "We're on a break. I don't want to think about your business."

"Well someone has to." Andrew sounded hurt. He stood up. "Let's go. We've still got four cats to feed."

They put the dogs away in silence and got on their bikes, riding up Grove Avenue. After the cats were fed, Andrew turned on an automatic sprinkler system and they pedaled toward home on the streets below the Boulevard. At a tiny corner store Andrew stopped to talk to one of his customers while Sally waited, looking through people's front gardens into their back yards, wondering if under some oak or dogwood tree she would see Zorro's men's horses, moving restlessly while they waited for their masters. Maybe Zorro himself would appear, looking toward Sally. He would raise his hand. "Wait," he would call as he cantered up to her, wheeling his horse to a stop. He would be smiling and very handsome, and she would give him a level look.

A wailing siren interrupted her thoughts. Two police cars burst into sight, sirens bleating in short bursts as they whizzed by. Andrew hurried out of the store, peering up the street as another police car wailed around a corner with its lights flashing.

"Something big's happened." He hopped on his bike. "They're on the Boulevard."

They pedaled fast, rounding the corner to see a cluster of police cars in front of the museum.

"Six cruisers!" Andrew said.

Sally coasted slowly along the curb beside him, taking in the squawking loudspeakers, the police dogs and handlers coming in and out of the shrubbery around the building. The sky was lit by huge arc lights, bugs fluttering in their glare.

"We better get Mom," Sally said.

"Mom's already here." Andrew pointed to the wide entrance, where she stood in the glare of the searchlights, talking to three police officers. "This looks really bad."

Even from far off Sally and Andrew could tell how upset their mother was – her usually cheerful face looked almost gray under the lights. They locked their bikes to the rack by the steps and pushed through the crowd to reach her. She tried to smile at them, but it didn't quite work.

"It's clear that several of the toys are gone, Mrs. Corbett," one of the officers was saying. "But we aren't sure exactly which ones until you show us." His name badge read Miller. He had a neatly- trimmed mustache and graying hair underneath his hat.

"Do you have any idea what happened? How the thieves got in?" Mom asked as they all walked inside.

"Not yet," the other policeman, a younger officer named Knudsen, said. "We're not sure if there's been negligence or…" He glanced at Miller, who was shaking his head like he didn't want his partner to say anything more.

Sally saw her mother's face tighten. Could they mean this was Mom's fault?

Sally wondered which toys were gone. The tin circus train pulled by two wind-up elephants, with tin boxes that fitted on the train cars and opened into animal cages with all the toy lions and tigers inside? The Pullman train, complete with seats that turned into beds with tiny sheets and blankets and pillows, even net hammocks for the clothes? She, Andrew and Jane knew every toy by heart, watching their mother work day after day, her staff carefully unpacking each toy as it arrived. Just this week they'd begun designing the glass display cases that looked like small-scale rooms or gardens, with lifelike figures of children playing with the toys.

Now she almost hated to walk through the marble halls, darker than usual, and across the indoor courtyard planted with trees. Even its usually splashing fountain was quiet, as if it was sad as well.

Two of the officers began going in and out of the other

exhibit rooms, with one of the museum guards turning lights on and off as they went, their voices echoing.

At the end of the passage Mrs. Corbett turned down a private hall towards an open door, where two more policemen stood in the middle of a large storage room. Everyone waited, silent, while Mom began to walk along the big tables, torn open crates and broken glass display cases, seeing how the children's figures inside had been knocked over, their careful settings strewn every which way.

A door banged and Sally heard the sound of footsteps hurrying toward them. A tall, ruddy-faced man in a seersucker blazer hurried into the room. "I came as soon as I heard," he said, sounding a little out of breath. "Cary, what happened? The policeman on the phone said—"

"And you are, sir?" Miller asked.

"Robert Calhoun, the museum's Executive Director." He held out his hand to shake Miller's before he took in the destroyed room. "A robbery. Here? Cary, how did this happen?" He pulled out a handkerchief and wiped his perspiring face. Mom stepped forward. "It seems someone broke in...they were able to bypass the main alarm."

"What?!" The museum director's voice was rising.

"Let me bring you up to date, sir," Miller said calmly. "We were just going through the room more thoroughly. Mrs. Corbett, can you tell us how much is gone?"

Mom had been inspecting the damage while Miller

spoke. At the end of the room she turned around. "It's hard to tell yet," she said. "But certainly quite a few of the smaller toys." Her voice shook a little, and Sally thought she was on the edge of tears.

"Would you say it was methodical?" Miller asked.

"Oh, yes, very methodical," Mom answered. "They must have known exactly what they wanted, and they were going after it – until they triggered the secondary alarm."

"Was the exhibit properly armed? Who's job is it to check that?" Miller spoke calmly, but Sally felt herself tense. She glanced at Andrew, who was looking down at the floor and scowling. Neither of them liked where this was going.

"It's my job, when I'm the last to leave," Mom said. "And yes, the alarm was on. And as I'm sure you know, you can check that with the security company."

Sally breathed a sigh of relief. She hadn't thought of that.

"Right," Miller said, nodding, and writing down the company's name.

Mom's glance veered to a box in the middle of a table. "Strange," she said slowly, "Here, the thieves left some of the better things. I'll have to get my inventory list – but here I think they misjudged..." she was walking along, rapidly now, "...and yes, here too." She turned, looking puzzled. "Not the most expert choices, then."

"What does that mean?" Miller asked. He tapped

his pen against his notepad.

Mom frowned. "I don't know. That they were amateurs, perhaps." She turned and looked around the room. "No, not amateurs. But it is odd."

"We have a report from a guard that he might have seen someone inside after closing," Officer Knudsen said. "But when he went to look he couldn't find anyone.

Mom looked at him. "So there was someone inside earlier," she said. "And he must have been very clever."

Sally was watching Mr. Calhoun pace up and down the room, avoiding the broken glass and open crates on the ground. He wasn't just the executive director. He was mom's boss, and now a robbery had ruined her exhibit...

"We saw someone hanging around this afternoon," Andrew broke in. "It was outside, and half a block away, but we noticed him because he was wearing a heavy canvas jacket with lots of pockets and a headlamp. A guy on a motorcycle."

Sally shivered, remembering the guy's hard, cold stare.

"Could you give us a description? Of him or the motorcycle?" Miller was asking. "Every bit of information helps."

Sally let Andrew do most of the talking, and she listened closely as he described everything he could remember about the man, the motorcycle, and how he had sped away when he saw them watching him. "He looked mean," Sally added. "The way he stared at me gave me the creeps."

Miller folded his pad. "This sounds like it could fit with the other reports."

"I could help you look for him," Andrew said. "I do people's yards and keep an eye on their houses, so I'm used to surveillance work."

Officer Knudsen grinned. "Thanks, buddy," he said. "But it would be best if you stay out of it. If these are professionals they are likely dangerous." He turned to Mrs. Corbett. "When will you be able to give us a full inventory?"

Mom glanced at her boss. "I'll have it done by 10 AM tomorrow," she said. "If that's all, I'll leave you to your work."

Mr. Calhoun followed them into the hallway. "I don't need to tell you how serious this is, Cary." He pursed his lips.

"No, you don't," Mom agreed. "But I'm sure the police will get to the bottom of it, and they have some good leads."

Sally thought Mom was trying to sound more reassuring than she felt, and Mr. Calhoun shook his head.

"Even so, it's a disaster — not only for our reputation, but for all the collectors who trusted us to keep their heirlooms safe, not to mention the other museums who added so much to this exhibit." He sighed deeply. "I'll contact the board of Directors immediately." He nodded to Andrew and Sally before he strode away.

Mom leaned against the wall and closed her eyes. Sally and Andrew exchanged glances and went over to hug her.

"Mom, it's going to be OK," Andrew said. His voice cracked and he cleared his throat. "They'll find the toys."

Mom straightened her back and put an arm around each of them. "Thank you. But it's not just the toys. The Board took a big chance, making me the Head Curator. Having Mr. Calhoun question my competence doesn't help. Although," she looked away for a minute, "he never was enthusiastic about this exhibit. He might not mind if it fails and I lose my job."

"But we'd mind," Andrew said as they started walking along the hallway. "And everyone else would. It can't fail."

"How could anybody have done something so awful?" Sally burst out. "All those beautiful toys! Why would anyone want to ruin something so important?"

They reached the museum's entrance and went outside, squinting in the glare of the spotlights.

"Thank you so much, officers," Mom said to the policemen as they passed. "The staff and I appreciate anything you can do."

Then she turned back to Sally and her face looked sad. "Lots of people do things like this – sometimes just to vandalize, to be destructive – but often for the money. They don't care about beauty, about history…" she trailed off, thinking. Then she began again. "But some of those toys are irreplaceable, and if we don't get them back, that will truly break my heart."

Andrew touched her arm again. "We'll help, Mom. I promise. There's got to be something we can do." He wasn't going to let anything more happen to the family — and he was definitely not going to let Mom lose her job.

"There is something." Mom smiled at him. "Get your bikes and I'll follow you home. And then get a good night's sleep so we'll all have clear heads in the morning."

And, Sally said to herself, so we can figure out a way to get every last one of those toys back.

CHAPTER THREE

Across the city Henry Morrison got silently out of bed and crossed to the window. A rooster crowed, and he could see that along the river it was growing light. Church Hill, where the Morrisons lived, was an Historic District, and some people kept chickens, like old-fashioned times. Henry liked the rooster's sound — it reminded him of his grandmother's small house in the country.

It would be clear today and that meant it would be hot – he'd have a lot of watering to do later, in his clients' gardens. But for now the dawn breeze was cool as he found a tank top and shorts and picked up his running shoes, tiptoeing along the hall. His little sister Rose was still asleep in the room next to his, and his parents' room was quiet too. But Fluffy, the family's Australian sheepdog, stood waiting downstairs, her short tail waggling so hard it moved her hind legs back and forth.

"How do you always know when I'm going running?" Henry tousled her ears while he pulled on his shoes. Outside the sun was peeping gold over the trees at the top of the hill when Henry walked his bike across the yard, marveling at how many birds were singing at the same time. He loved the way they sounded on early summer mornings, not singing their hearts out the way they did in the spring, but full of life just the same.

"I guess I just like bird noises," he said to Fluffy as he hopped on his bike.

She answered him with a quick yap, running on ahead while he pedaled slowly to where Church Hill dropped off, looking south to the river and west to Broad Street. His glance dipped down into the Shockoe ravine and then up again to the business section of the city. He could see the red clay gashes where huge cranes had torn up the trees that had lined each side of the ravine. Henry hated the way the cranes looked, reaching for the sky, and the way they had destroyed the trees.

"Not that you'd notice," he said to Fluffy. "The only time you look at a tree is when a squirrel is running up it." He grinned at her and she gave his hand a quick nuzzle. Then he started up again, coasting down the hill and pedaling hard up the next. He was heading for the parking garage at the bottom of Main Street where the city's Marathon always had its finish line. When he reached it, he chained his bike to a stanchion inside, went back outside to stretch for a few minutes, and then, with Fluffy beside him, began to run.

Five miles to the west Sally woke up with a start, as if she'd just had a bad dream. She sat up quickly, wondering why she felt so nervous, but then it all rushed back – the robbery, the wreckage in the museum storerooms, and the look on her mother's face.

Early red-gold sunbeams were slanting in her window, a cardinal was calling outside, and insects were zinging their dawn songs. Usually some of her favorite noises, but not today. Nothing felt right today.

Wondering if anyone else was up, she got out of bed and went in the bathroom to splash water on her face. Then she walked to her door and stood listening, but the house was quiet. Hopefully her exhausted mom was still asleep. She went back to her dresser and pulled on a T-shirt and shorts. If she hurried, she could get in a run before everyone else woke up, which would clear her head. She knew that's what Dad would have done. He loved running, and because of him, she did too. He used to run whenever he felt upset about something, saying it helped him think better. And right now she needed to think better too.

Her bare feet made no sound padding down the back steps to the pantry, where Peaches came up to twine around her ankles. She stooped to pour some food into the cat's bowl. She grabbed a banana before writing a quick note to mom that she'd gone running, her mind still seeing the broken crates in the Museum's storeroom and scattered toys lying in the smashed glass cases. Walking across their house's thick straw rugs to the front door, she wondered again how anything so bad could happen to their mom, to them all.

"The toys might be in somebody's van right now, on their way to be sold in New York or someplace farther away than that," she'd said to Andrew last night when they were getting ready for bed.

"They could still be in Richmond, too," Andrew had answered, splashing water on his face, which was how he washed when Mom wasn't around. "And I've been thinking. Remember that guy on the motorcycle had really big jacket pockets? If he was one of the people they said was in the museum later, he could have stuffed the small toys in his pockets and got them out that way."

"And no one would notice anything," Sally said, as she reached for her toothbrush, feeling a quick shiver. She still didn't like thinking about the man on the motorcycle.

Andrew picked up his towel and dried his face. "Right. But whoever took them and wherever they are, the main thing is we have to get them back. And I'm not stopping until we do."

Last night his determination had made her feel better. But this morning, opening the heavy front door and trotting down the wide front steps in the early daylight with everything looking so familiar, she wasn't so sure. What, actually, could they do? They couldn't just hop on their bikes and pedal around the city streets, not knowing where to look. And they had so little time – the exhibit's opening date was only a few weeks away. Mom couldn't borrow any more toys, because after what had happened no one would trust the museum to keep them safe.

Worse still, since she was in charge, she was going to get blamed, even though it wasn't her fault. Sally swallowed hard. It wasn't what Mom needed, what any of them needed, coming on top of losing Dad. Sally brushed away the tears she felt welling up and reached for a Kleenex, then blew her nose and shoved her damp tissues back inside her shorts' pocket.

She crossed to the grass plot and did a few stretches before she started moving at a slow trot, hoping this would help her mood, her pace quickening when she breathed in a smell she loved – newly cut grass, its sweet scent mixed with damp earth. On the next block she let her speed pick up, running in and out of slanting sunbeams that flickered through the maples' trunks and turned the leaves vivid green.

She had gone four blocks when she noticed someone halfway up the grassplot ahead of her. A boy, running in bright blue shorts and a white tank, with a big blue-mottled dog keeping a steady lope beside him.

How long had he been there? She hadn't even noticed. That was so typical. No wonder her soccer coach kept telling her she was always daydreaming. As she slowed at the curb she saw something in the gutter. It looked like a swim-club patch, and she hesitated, breaking her stride. Could the boy ahead of her have dropped it? She swung in a circle and scooped up the patch.

It probably wasn't his, but it wouldn't hurt to find

out. He was going faster, and Sally relaxed her arms and hunched into her stride, leaning slightly forward, churning along the dappled grass with big drops of dew splashing over her flying feet.

She looked up just in time to see the boy swerving out and slowing, looking startled. He was African-American, probably a year or so older than she was. His dog circled too, looking at them attentively.

"Sorry, hi, wait…" she panted, trying not to gulp air. "I found this." She waved her hand with the patch in it. "I thought it might be yours."

He looked surprised. "Hey…it is! I must have dropped it. Thanks a lot." He turned the patch over in his hand. "I just got it, in a race. That'll teach me to sew 'em on better."

He smiled at her, and Sally saw other patches, up and down the side of his shorts.

"You race?" He gestured for her to use the path, and fell in beside her, jogging slowly. Sally noticed he was breathing easily, his stride springy and relaxed, while she was still catching her breath.

"No," she said. "I just like running. And it keeps me fast for soccer and lacrosse."

"Anybody as fast as you ought to race too," he said.

"Really?" Sally heard her voice squeak.

"I was motoring," he said. "You had to be flying to catch up. What's your mile time?"

"I don't know. I've never timed myself." She looked

again at his patches. "It looks like you win a lot."

He nodded. "In my category, 13 and under. I want to do more, though. I'm training for a half-marathon this October. I'm hoping to win my age group."

They had reached the top of the block and he pointed to a street, lined with tall oak trees. "Here's my route. Thanks again for my patch. I really appreciate that."

With a wave he veered off, his dog alongside, and Sally turned around too, realizing that for a few minutes she'd forgotten the robbery. Then it all came back in a rush, along with a feeling of dread. Mom would be up by now, and Sally hated to think what she'd find.

But at the house Mom seemed calm. She was sitting in the kitchen with Andrew and Jane, who were gobbling down wheat puffs. And though her eyes had purplish half-circles under them, like she hadn't slept much, she could even smile at her oldest daughter.

"I'm glad you're back," she said. "There's one bit of good news. I just heard from the Lieutenant that the alarm was turned on, obviously by me, when I left the museum last night."

"That's great!" Sally said. She put her arms around her mother and hugged her. "And," Mom went on, "the Lieutenant also said the alarm was turned off again about an hour and a half later, from the inside."

"You know what that means," Andrew looked up from his cereal bowl. "One of the burglars stayed there."

Their mother nodded. "And he would have been an

expert about electronic systems. The police now think these are professionals who were looking the museum over and studying our security system long before the robbery."

"But where would a burglar hide so the guards wouldn't see him?" Jane asked. She looked worried.

"It's a big museum," Andrew said. "And there aren't as many guards on duty after everyone leaves, right Mom?"

"That's right." Their mother looked at her watch. "Anyway I'll learn more when I get there. Right now I have to go. The press is already parked in front of the building, and I'm meeting with my staff members in thirty minutes." She stood up and looked at Andrew and Sally. "I'm sure I'll need to stay at the museum most of the day, so if you two will come to my office at lunchtime we'll get sandwiches in the cafeteria."

They nodded, and she turned to Jane, who was pushing a biscuit around her plate. "Time to leave. Not good to be late your first day at summer school. You can take that biscuit with you."

Jane got up and carefully pushed in her chair before she rushed out behind Mom, and Andrew stood up too. "I've got some ideas about clues we can start on as soon as we get the pigeons done and get to the museum," he said to Sally. "Catch up with me at Kelso's?"

She nodded. She was wondering how Mom could stay so calm. I want to be like her some day, she thought, as Mac came in with a saucepan full of lukewarm oatmeal. She spooned it into a bowl, which Sally filled to the top with milk and brown sugar.

"It's good you're helping your brother," Mac said. "It's just wonderful a boy that age, trying so hard. When I was little all we did was work, but nowadays most young people don't do anything. Why, years ago…"

Sally's mind glazed over while Mac went on talking. Even though she understood Mac's special feeling for Andrew – liking the business world, as she said, 'the same as me' – Mac's lectures on the old days could go on and on.

Sally concentrated on finishing her cereal before she said, "Maybe they know something by now."

Mac nodded. "Let's hope." She patted Sally's shoulder. "Your mom's a good woman. This shouldn't have happened to her."

For the second time that morning, Sally's eyes filled with tears. She blinked hard. "It's just that we've got to help her, and I don't know what to do."

Mac reached for a paper napkin and handed it to Sally.

"Just what you *are* doing," she said. "Helping Andrew, so you'll both have more time to help your mother. And keeping your hopes up, which will make her do the same. Things could still turn out for the best."

Sally managed a lopsided smile. That was what Mac always said, and even though today it was hard to believe, it somehow made Sally feel better. Maybe, she thought as she hopped on her bike, Andrew's idea about clues would make sense too.

Mr. Kelso's pigeons were flying in a wide circle above the rooftops when Sally reached his house. For a minute she stood still, entranced, watching them climb higher and higher into the sky.

"I've cleaned their boxes and filled their food and water trays," Andrew called from inside their coop "That'll hold them 'til later."

He stepped out, carrying a tin pie plate full of seeds. As he held it up and rattled it the pigeons, far up, either heard the sound or saw his form by the coop, arm upstretched. The whole flock turned, and almost as one bird they hurtled down like arrows, banking and slipping through the air without stopping until they landed on the coop's roof and pushed their way in through the hanging wire doors, heading straight for the feed trays.

"That's amazing!" Sally said. "I never knew pigeons were so smooth!"

"They're homing pigeons. They've been trained to come in fast to save time in a race," Andrew said. "And right now, we need to hurry too."

Henry leaned his bike against his back porch and walked into his house, heading for the kitchen. He washed his hands and took a croissant from a tray his father was pulling from the oven, chewing while he picked up his orange juice.

"How'd it go?" His father asked.

"Fine," Henry said. "I did a 5:35, and it felt okay."

His father, a lawyer who had been a champion track and fielder in college, trained Henry in his spare time. He eyed Henry over the top of his bifocals. "Okay."

Henry sighed. He knew that his father's "okay" really meant not okay. There were many times when what he did wasn't enough for his dad.

"See if you can break 5:30 next week." Mr. Morrison began arranging the croissants on a plate.

"Dad, I'm trying." Henry couldn't keep the frustration out of his voice. "I'll leave earlier tomorrow before the heat comes up. Maybe I can shave five seconds off."

Mr. Morrison looked up from the platter. "As you should have been doing all along."

Henry stared at the croissants and took a deep breath. "Yeah, okay," he said.

"By the way, there was a big robbery in the West End last night. Antique toys from the Museum. Very valuable, some of them." Mr. Morrison was Chairman of the museum's Board of Trustees and also volunteered his legal services. "I'm headed there later to see what I can do. Tell your mother I had to leave early, will you? She and Rose are out walking."

"Right," Henry said, picking up another croissant, covering it with honey and washing it down with a second glass of orange juice. He ran upstairs to change, left a note for his mother, snapped his key pouch to his belt and patted Fluffy goodbye. Then he hopped on his bike and pedaled along East Broad Street into the now steaming morning.

He passed the eastern side of Church Hill and came to Chimborazo Park — a neighborhood of older brick houses with brick-walled gardens — where he had several clients. He worked fast until noon, cutting grass and trimming walks and shrubs, finally stopping to spray water from a hose over his head and down his T-shirt. He stood for a few minutes in the cool stream before he put his cap back on and walked his bike along a cobbled alley. At the end he pushed open a high, ramshackle gate, actually a collection of slats nailed together by two wide boards, centered in a run-down fence.

But once inside, the garden was surprising. A small but carefully tended square of deep green grass lay in the middle of flower borders filled with exotic plants, surrounded by a walkway of bricks. At the outer edges of the yard, tall magnolia trees shaded stone benches in the cool spaces underneath.

My wonderful garden, Henry thought to himself. Of course it wasn't his, it was his client's, but since Henry had helped plant it, he still felt that way. He always tried to leave it for last because it was so special. All the plants, shrubs and flowers were endangered varieties, preserved and grown, as his client, a professor, liked to say, by "nuts like me who keep them going." From the professor, Henry had learned how to prune and water, thin and transplant these unusual plants, and the more he worked with them, the more interested he became. It was as though all his yard work had led to this wondrous new world called Botany, a world he wanted to explore more and more.

Now, closing the gate, Henry stepped onto the bricks and waved at the professor, who was sitting on the porch. "Hello, sir. How are you?"

"Oh, not bad for an old history professor."

It was what he always said, and Henry grinned. He didn't seem old, although he had been a history professor, even a famous one, according to Henry's dad. That was before he'd retired from William and Mary College in Williamsburg and come back to Richmond. Henry wasn't sure what he was doing now besides taking care of his plants, but it really didn't matter – working with him in this garden was enough.

Now the Professor put away what he was holding and came down the steps, pointing to a plant halfway down the border.

"I've been looking at the *Cypripedium*," he said, heading along the brick path.

Henry knew that was the Latin name for Lady Slippers plants, and he crouched down to look at the pink and white flowers. Puffing slightly, the professor bent beside him. "They're used to the heat, but I think they all need more dappled shade than they've got, with this July sun right overhead at mid-day. We need to move them."

"Right," Henry said, and set to work carefully, loosening the soil around the Lady Slippers' roots while the professor watched.

"Excellent," he said, patting Henry on the shoulder. "You have a gift with plants, my boy."

Henry smiled, carefully lifting the Lady Slipper from the soil while Professor Saunders walked up and down the border peering up at the sun's angle in the sky. Finally he found a spot that satisfied him and tapped the earth with his fingers.

"Here," he said. "If you'll bring the nutrient bag from the porch, I'll dig. It's next to those boxes with the blue plastic covers."

Henry ran up the porch steps and looked around. He saw the bag of plant food but when he reached to pick it up, his foot accidentally touched one of the boxes and something fell out with a clatter. Henry jumped, but it was only a flat piece of wood with two small wheels, shaped like a horse.

"Leave that alone!" the Professor called quickly. "Come back here and get some water, these plants are already drooping." Then in a calmer voice he added, "I'll add the nutrients later."

It was not until later that afternoon that Henry

would remember thinking it odd that an unmarried, elderly history professor had a wooden child's pull toy, with its paint peeling off, on his back porch.

CHAPTER FOUR

When Sally and Andrew walked into their mother's office she was sitting at her desk, surrounded by papers.

"You're early!" She said, getting up to give them each a quick hug, but not picking up the ringing phone on her desk.

"We finished what we had to do," Andrew said.

"Has anything more happened?" Sally added.

"Well, yes," Mom sat back down. "Something puzzling. We realized that all the toys were made of wood. And they were all from the late 1700s."

Andrew frowned. "What do you think that means?" he said.

Mom shrugged. "We're not sure yet, but it's strange that the thieves left some really valuable toys behind."

"1700s," Sally said. "That's the time of the American Revolution, isn't it?"

"It is." Mom was interrupted by a knock on the door, and a voice saying "Cary?"

They turned to see a tall, distinguished-looking man standing in the doorway, wearing gray slacks and a crisp blue shirt.

"Jim! I'm so glad to see you!" Mom stood up again to shake hands.

"And I you." He glanced at Sally and Andrew.

"These are my children," Mom went on. "They've taken time off from their lawn business to help me."

Mr. Morrison smiled at them. "Good for you," he said. "I should get you together with my son – he has lawn jobs too, and he's snowed under, mostly from spending too much time in one client's garden. If I can find him, I'll bring him with me when I come back for the press conference this afternoon."

"Great," Andrew said. "Maybe we can go in business together."

"Not a bad idea." Mr. Morrison smiled again and sat down in a small armchair beside a table overflowing with books. It was one of the only chairs in Mom's office that didn't have a stack of reports or museum catalogs on it. "But right now your mother and I need to plan what I say to the press about this terrible robbery." His face had turned serious. "I want the public to know it was not your mother's fault. She's a fine curator and she's been handling the project really well. The robbery happened because the thieves were able to bypass our aging security system."

"Thank you," Mom said to him, and to Sally and Andrew she said, "why don't I see you at the cafeteria at noon? I'm sure you can find things to do 'til then?"

"Yes," Sally said. "We'll be fine."

"Okay," Andrew said in the hall, "We can start in the storeroom."

They hurried, passing a group of school-aged children wearing matching T-shirts who had stopped to stare at some bright neon lights hanging from a gallery ceiling, looking like a giant eggbeater.

"I think it's supposed to be a comet," Andrew said, pushing past the group.

One of the guards told them not to run in the hallways, but no one noticed when they slipped through a side door marked "Employees Only" and went down the deserted passage. "If anyone stops us, we'll tell them we're helping Mom," Andrew whispered.

The forensic technicians had blocked off the storeroom door with yellow tape, but inside the toys still lay where they'd been thrown, a few on the tables but mostly scattered around the floor. Each one's position was marked with chalk.

"It looks so sad," Sally whispered.

"It's a crime scene," Andrew said, ducking under the tape. "Come on. Clues."

He hurried to the empty cases of the room but Sally stopped. "How'll we know what's a clue?" she said.

"Just guess." Andrew pulled a pencil and a small red notebook out of his pocket. It was the notebook where he kept his pet care instructions, and he never went anywhere without it. "We have to start somewhere."

He was already across the room when they both heard an odd tapping sound. Sally looked over to see a man standing in the hallway, just outside the crime tape.

He was wearing dark aviator glasses and moving a cane up and down the sides of the doorway, as if he was trying to figure out what it was. Suddenly she realized why – the man was blind. He had long blond hair hanging down his back, and he stood uncertainly, almost weaving from side to side. He seemed to sense someone else was there.

"Who is it?" he called in a loud, gruff voice.

"We're working in here," Andrew answered as Sally walked closer. "Are you looking for someone? Visitors aren't allowed in this part of the museum."

"You sound like a kid," the man said, a twisted smile on his face. "If visitors aren't allowed, what're you doing here?"

"Our mother is a curator and we're working for her," Sally said, wondering why the man was making her uneasy. "And my brother asked you, what are you doing here? Are you looking for the main entrance?"

For a minute the man's face reddened and he scowled, but then he made another effort to smile. "Okay. I guess I'm lost. How far is it?"

Andrew slipped under the tape. "I'll take you," he said, putting his hand on the man's bare arm.

"Don't touch me!" The man shouted, giving Andrew a hard shove. "Don't I look like I can walk? Just stay beside me and tell me to go straight or turn, things like that."

Andrew forced himself to take a deep breath. "Okay," he said. "Just turn around and go straight ahead. I'll walk

with you." He called to Sally. "See you in a minute."

Ten minutes later he was back, looking puzzled. "That was weird," he said.

"He was probably just lost." Sally looked up from where she was squatting on the floor in front of a broken case.

"No, I mean, he was wearing a watch. I saw it when I tried to take his arm. If he was blind, why would he wear a watch? He couldn't see it to tell time."

"Maybe someone gave it to him," she said. "Anyway, I'm just about finished. All I found was a wad of dried-up chewing gum." She held it up.

"Not much of a clue." Andrew sounded disappointed. "This isn't getting us anywhere."

"You're right. We need to figure out a better way." Sally said, "But right now we need to meet Mom."

Mom was already at the cafeteria, standing in line. The cafeteria was one of Sally's favorite places, with glass walls that filtered the sunlight and a view of the museum's beautiful gardens.

"So tell me what you saw this morning," Mom said, after they'd found a table and sat down with their food.

"Neon lights," Sally said.

"Some of it was cool." Andrew added. He had ordered a large grilled cheese and tomato sandwich with fries, and was busy pouring ketchup all over it. Mom, watching, shook her head, while Sally bit into her chickpea and sprout sandwich.

"I've been thinking about the robbers taking only the wooden toys," Sally said, taking a swallow of her lemonade. "What could have been so special about them?"

"They're very old, for one thing." Their mother finished her gazpacho soup and put down her spoon. "Pretty much the oldest ones in the exhibit. That makes them very valuable."

Andrew had been dipping his fries in a puddle of ketchup, but now he looked thoughtful. "But what did kids do with them? They didn't have any batteries, or anything electric, did they?"

Mrs. Corbett rolled her eyes. "Andrew! No, they didn't have batteries, and no screens either."

Sally could see where this was going – a lecture by Mom about too much screen time – so she rushed on, "Actually, I like the old toys. I like the way they feel when you pick them up."

Andrew finished munching his sandwich and wiped his mouth. "But what did they do without electronic stuff like games?"

"What children have always done until your gadgets came along," Mom said. "They pretended. They used their imaginations and made up games or other things to do with their toys."

Sally saw the Museum Director coming toward them and she nudged Mom, who turned around in her chair. Today he wore a light blue blazer with a navy bow tie.

"This robbery shouldn't have happened, Cary," Mr. Calhoun said, after he shook hands with Andrew and Sally.

Mom was about to say something, but her boss cut in. "I've learned that some of the collectors may be threatening to..." He was interrupted by an assistant rushing over to tell him he had an urgent phone call, and he left their table saying goodbye over his shoulder.

"What does he think the collectors are going to do?" Andrew sprinkled more salt on his french fries.

Mom sighed. "He's worried some of them will file a lawsuit against us. If they do, the museum will have to fire me because I'm the Head Curator. It's like the captain going down with the ship."

Sally's eyes grew rounder and she put down her sandwich. All of a sudden, she didn't feel hungry anymore. "If you can find the toys and get them back, would the collectors still sue?"

Mom shook her head. "Probably not, if the toys aren't damaged."

"We're going to find the toys. Andrew and I have already started working on it," Sally said.

"Let the police do that, please." Mom sipped her iced tea. "Now let's finish eating. I have calls to make before the press conference."

Mr. Morrison was already in Mom's office, and when Sally saw who was with him, her eyes opened wide.

"I know you!" She and the boy said at the same

time. "We saw each other this morning, when we were running!" Sally explained to everyone. "I'm Sally," she smiled at him.

"Well, to be formal, this is Henry." Mr. Morrison smiled too.

"And I'm Andrew," Andrew stepped forward. "I'm the one with the lawn business."

"I've heard," Henry grinned. "I think my father wants us to team up."

"Only an idea you two can explore," Mr. Morrison said. He looked at Mom. "Did you learn anything more?"

She shook her head.

"But I'd better not say the robbery was only wooden toys from the late 1700s," Mr. Morrison said,

"Please don't," Mom said. "Why tell the thieves we've figured that out?"

"And I'll stick to talking about the exhibit's importance," Mr. Morrison finished.

They were interrupted by an assistant saying the television crew had arrived and were setting up their cameras in the main hall. When they had all walked in, Sally, Andrew and Henry moved back to the edge of the room.

"What was your mom saying about the thieves only taking certain kinds of toys?" Henry asked in a low voice.

Andrew told him what Mom had said, and Henry looked thoughtful. "Wooden," he said. "And old," he added, as though it wasn't a question.

"Yes. They're all antiques," Sally said.

Henry murmured something, and Andrew's ears pricked up. "What's wrong?"

Henry drew in a deep breath. "I'm not sure," he said. "But I was at a client's house this morning, and something I saw made me think…" he stopped, watching their faces. "…it made me think one of the toys might be on his back porch," he finished, talking very fast.

They stared at him.

"Seriously?" Andrew said.

"Look, I'm not positive – I said might be. I didn't get that good a look at it." Henry was looking across the room at his father, who stood with the TV anchor.

"We've got to tell Mom and your dad, right now," Sally said.

"NO!" Henry's voice was almost a shout, and one of the news crew turned, his finger to his lips. "Not until I go back to his house and check," he said more softly.

"Listen," Sally whispered, while across the room the TV Anchor stepped forward, beaming at Mr. Morrison. "This whole exhibit is our mother's project. It's the first exhibit she's ever had. It's not her fault the toys got stolen, but she's getting the blame. And the people who loaned the toys will think the museum can't protect its exhibits, and she might lose her job and our dad died last year, and…" Sally's eyes were welling up, but Andrew finished for her. "So," he whispered, "we have to help get the toys back, and we're going to, even though our mom told us to let the police handle it."

Sally stared at Henry. "You've got to tell us what you know," she said.

"I know this professor is one of my best and kindest clients," Henry whispered back. "And I'm not saying anything to anybody 'til I'm sure."

"Professor?" Andrew said.

"Yes," Henry said, "but I repeat, I'm not saying anything until I go back and check."

They stood looking at each other until Andrew let out his breath. "Okay. What if we go to your client's house and look at whatever you saw. If it's one of the museum toys, we'll tell our parents, and if it's not we won't have gotten everybody's hopes up."

At that moment a big light illuminated the platform that had been set up in the center of the room, and Mr. Morrison stepped into the glare. The TV anchor, a young woman, walked forward and smiled at the cameras, lined up in a row.

"Good evening," she began. "I'm Peggy Brown and I'm speaking to you from the great hall of the Virginia Museum of Fine Arts, where a major robbery took place last night. With me is Mr. James Morrison, Chairman of the Board of the Museum."

She turned to Henry's dad. "I'd like to tell the viewers about these toys," she said. "Anything special about them?"

"They're all very special to their owners, and to us,

here at the museum. They tell a wonderful story of how children lived and played, a long time ago," Mr. Morrison said as slides began to scroll across the big monitor.

"See if you recognize anything," Sally whispered to Henry.

He watched intently, and as a flat pull-toy shaped like a horse flashed across the screen, he pointed. "It might have been that," he said. "Or one like it."

"Okay," Andrew said. "We've got our bikes here. Let's get moving."

Sally could see Henry hesitate, and she smiled at him. "Look, we really know what all the toys look like, better than you do."

"And," Andrew grinned, "I'd like to see what that professor's yard looks like – how you do your business."

"You mean see the competition?" Henry half smiled, and spread his hands out in front of him. "Okay, I'll take you. My bike's here, in my dad's car. Let's go."

Outside the afternoon heat was building, probably to a thunderstorm later, Andrew thought. The air felt like a blanket as they left the air-conditioned museum, but once they were under the Fan District's big shade trees, they could feel a slight breeze. They headed east on quieter streets and in another twenty minutes they were pulling up the hill to Chimborazo Park, its flat expanse dotted with sprinklers sending sprays of water across the grass. Henry coasted into the cobblestone alley and hopped off to walk until he reached the rickety fence.

"This is it," he said in a low voice. "He usually goes out in the afternoons. Wait here." He went through the gate while Sally and Andrew leaned their bikes against the fence.

"Church Hill's a great neighborhood," Andrew whispered. "Did you notice all the front gardens?"

Sally nodded, pulling off her bike helmet and lifting the hair off her neck. "The two of you could really expand if you figured out how."

"I'm thinking about it," Andrew said. We…" He stopped as the gate opened and Henry came out, frowning.

"I can't find the toy, at least not where it fell, and I don't want to look like I'm snooping. I dropped my cap behind some stuff on the porch, so I'll have an excuse to come back in the morning and look some more."

"Sharp," Andrew said. "What time should we meet? We could be here by…" he thought, "8:30?"

Henry looked back at the house, and they could tell he still wasn't happy. "I like the professor so much I'd hate it if he's actually got one of those toys. I'm almost sorry I said anything." But then he grinned suddenly, at Sally. "8:30 kind of knocks out a run, doesn't it?"

She laughed. "I don't think missing one day'll hurt us."

"See you tomorrow, then." He climbed back on his bike. "Right here."

"So, what do you think?" Andrew panted, perspiration dripping down his face as they rode beside the rush-hour traffic on their way back up Broad Street.

"He'll help, I can tell." Sally said. She looked back at a car that had swerved too close. "It's just so risky to wait."

CHAPTER FIVE

At supper Mom announced she had news. "Lieutenant Miller's team found something in the grass outside the museum — heavy string from one of the pull toys. And they also found a motorcycle tire print nearby."

"Our guy!" Andrew said, his mouth full of Mac's juicy fried chicken.

"Maybe." Mom put her hand to her mouth, meaning he should stop talking until he'd finished chewing. "But the Lieutenant doesn't think a professional thief would have been on a motorcycle. Professionals would have used a truck, or at least a van. And no antique toys have shown up for sale on the web sites we're watching."

"So it might be people who live here," Andrew said, getting up to turn on the window fan. The predicted thunderstorm had melted away, and the air had not cooled off. "And they could still be around."

"They could," Mom agreed. She picked up her fork. "I just hope all the news stories don't frighten them into taking the toys to Philadelphia or New York and selling them quickly."

"But couldn't the news be a good thing?" Andrew said, helping himself to another piece of cornbread from the basket Mac handed across the table. "It might make more people call the police if they see something."

"That's the hope." Mom looked over at Jane. "I haven't heard how summer school went," she said. "Did the glasses help?"

Jane nodded. "I liked it! I could read everything!" She almost shouted, sounding so excited everyone smiled at her.

"Wonderful." Mom said. Then she looked at Sally and Andrew. "And did you like Henry Morrison?"

"A lot," Andrew said. "He told us about some of his gardens. The trouble is, I'm not sure yet how we'd work together because he's pretty far away, on Church Hill. We're going over there in the morning to see, anyway."

That was true, even if it wasn't the whole truth, Sally thought. She spooned stewed tomatoes over her black-eyed peas, making a nice gloppy pile.

"Good," Mom said. "I need to go back to the Museum tonight to do paperwork. When you finish your jobs, please get to bed on time." They nodded and she looked at Jane. "And now that you can see to read, do your homework. Mac said she'll help if you need it, but please, don't argue."

For once, Jane didn't object. Everyone was pitching in, Sally thought. Even Mac had volunteered to skip night school classes if Mom needed her to stay home with them. And as Sally and Andrew rode their bikes down Grace Street after supper Sally noticed that he, like she, was watchful, looking in gardens, along alleys, down sidewalks, trying to see into any spaces holding parked motorcycles, alert to any big cardboard cartons or wooden crates nearby, anything big enough to hold a stash of wooden toys.

Andrew's voice cut into her thoughts. "I wish we knew exactly what the police found," he said coming up beside her as she was feeding a Dalmatian puppy, "I mean, where the tire print was, stuff like that."

"Me too," Sally said, while they walked back along the house to the sidewalk in front. Lightning bugs were flickering all around them, twinkling on and off like tiny stars above the grass.

"I thought of something else," Andrew said. "We should look up old wooden toys tonight. That's the best clue we have."

Sally climbed on her bike. "We promised Mom we'd go to bed on time."

"But we didn't promise we'd stay in bed." Andrew said. "We could get back up. And we might find something important."

"That is," he muttered an hour later, scrolling rapidly on his laptop while Sally stood guard at the hall door, listening for Mac. "If I can get on a good toy site "… tin, lead, wooden…" his cursor stopped.

Sally was peering down the hallway. "Hurry up. I don't want a long lecture from Mac if she sees your light on."

"Okay," Andrew said. "Hey! Get this! There's

a professor who lives in Richmond who studies the American Revolution, and…there was this whole spy ring working for George Washington during the Revolutionary War. This professor, his name's Montague Saunders…he thinks the spies hid their secret messages in things they found around the house, like toys."

"Seriously?" Sally came into the room to look over Andrew's shoulder.

Professor Montague Saunders was on the screen being interviewed, and Andrew tweaked the volume.

"And I am convinced," the professor was saying, "absolutely convinced, that messages were hidden in an object, something each one of them would have kept without arousing suspicion in his own household."

"Each one of who?" Sally said. "Is he talking about George Washington and those other guys?"

"I think so," Andrew said. There's also a Wikipedia article I was looking at." He pulled it up, and it said Professor Saunders was a famous historian who had spent many years studying the spy techniques used in the American Revolution. Back then people like Washington, Jefferson and Franklin hadn't been called our country's Founding Fathers. Instead their British rulers thought of them as rebels and traitors. If any one of them had been caught he would have been hanged, which meant they had to write each other in secret, and Professor Saunders believed they'd hidden their messages inside their children's wooden toys. He also suspected that some of those messages were still there in very old toys.

Sally and Andrew looked at each other. "We have to tell Henry," Sally said. "And see if this is the same professor."

"Henry's probably asleep right now," said Andrew. And we don't know if this has anything to do with the robbery. Even if that's the right professor and he has one of the toys, there's nothing we can do about it tonight."

After they went to bed, Sally lay for a long time on top of her sheets, something she liked to do when it was hot, thinking hard. If this professor did have the toys that would be why Henry couldn't find the one he'd seen this morning. And if he did, what should she and Andrew do?

Finally, her thoughts churning, she sat up, feeling a wild urge to jump from her window and run like the wind across the wet night grass. She would look for Zorro, and he would canter out of the dark shadows straight up to her, looking serious. "We need help," she would say, "and..."

Then she shook her head, frowning. "I'm being weird," she said aloud, stretching her legs and untangling her sheets. Shortly after, before she could think of anything more to worry about, she fell asleep.

In the morning when they came downstairs Mac was looking at the newspaper. Their mother's face was on the front page. The headline read 'Toy Exhibit Ruined, Head Curator Cary Corbett says.'

"I never said those words." Mom stared at her bowl of dry cereal. "Though that's certainly how I felt when the reporters asked me. They've twisted everything." She pushed her bowl away and stood up. "I'd better get going. I'm sure the museum's phones are blowing up."

Sally was on her way to the kitchen for orange juice but she stopped. "Should we come over later?"

"We have some work to do first," Andrew said in a quiet voice.

Their mother looked suspicious. "As long as none of it interferes with what the police are doing," she said.

"It won't," Andrew said, widening his eyes to look innocent.

As soon as Mom left they bolted their food and rushed out, jumping on their bikes and splitting up. Sally took one block of dogs and cats while Andrew took another, turning on sprinklers as he went. He fed Mr. Kelso's pigeons without letting them out and caught up with Sally on Hanover Avenue.

"It's eight o'clock," he said. "We can leave the sprinklers going 'til we get back."

Henry was waiting when they turned into the professor's alley, wearing a blue shirt with white letters that read Norfolk 5K Qualifier on the front.

"Perfect timing," he said. "I'll go in first and tell the professor I've come to get my cap. He won't mind if

I've got some friends with me, and that way we can look around together."

They nodded, and he slid inside the gate.

But he came back frowning. "He's still not answering, and when I knocked hard on the back door, it just swung open."

"I think we should come with you," Andrew said.

They pulled their bikes into a parking space at the end of the fence and edged through the gate, looking around. Sally could smell the magnolia blossoms, and she saw a big Blue Jay splashing in the birdbath. When they moved closer he flew off, startled, to a tree.

"This is beautiful!" She whispered.

"The professor's a great horticulturist," Henry said, keeping his voice low.

He led the way up the steps and stopped at the half-open door. "Here goes," he muttered.

"Right behind you," Andrew said.

They entered a cheerful sunroom with comfortable easy chairs and a plaid rug, lamps, and bookcases overflowing with books.

Henry took a deep breath and called, "Professor? Professor Saunders?" Sally and Andrew exchanged glances when they heard the name. "It's him," Sally mouthed silently at Andrew, who nodded.

Henry tried again, louder. "PROFESSOR?"
Now the silence was noticeable. A clock ticked on the mantle. A bird chirped outside.

Henry looked at them. "I don't like this," he said. "He's always here in the morning."

They moved silently across the floor to a door at the room's far side. Henry pushed it open, and they found themselves in a hall with windows looking onto the street in front. To their right was a staircase, curving up, and under it, crumpled on the floor, lay a man.

"Oh, no — Professor!" Henry rushed forward. Behind him, Sally's voice quivered. "Is he dead?"

But as Henry kneeled by the motionless figure, the man's eyes opened and looked at him. A trickle of blood from his head was pooling on the floor.

"Thank goodness you've come," the man whispered. Then his eyes closed again.

"Should I call 911?" Andrew asked, pulling out his phone.

Henry was reaching in his pocket for his. "Yes, and I'm calling my mom. We live near here. Can you stay with him a second?" he said to Sally.

She knelt down, just as the professor's eyes opened again. "They're gone," he whispered. "They took them all."

"Who?" Sally whispered back. "What did they take?"

But he didn't seem to hear. Henry crouched beside her, and Sally looked up.

"He said something," she told him. "He said, 'they took them all'." She saw Henry's puzzled look and added,

"he probably means the toys."

Henry's mouth tightened. "We don't know what he meant," he said. "So don't say anything. My mom's on her way."

"So's 911," Andrew said. "I'll stand out front so they can see us sooner."

But it was Mrs. Morrison who arrived first, jumping out of her car and running up the front steps. Instantly she squatted beside the professor. He was still breathing, but his face was very pale.

"Hello, dear," she said to Sally. "Sally, right? Could you please bring me a damp cloth from the kitchen." She sounded nice, like Henry, Sally thought as she ran a blue and white dishcloth under the faucet. She could hear the wails of an ambulance far off.

"We mustn't move him until they get here," Mrs. Morrison said, taking the dish towel from Sally and putting it gently on Professor Saunders' forehead. Again he opened his eyes, and she took his hand. "Help's on the way." She smiled at him.

Now they heard more sirens, sounding louder, coming closer, and then two paramedics were running up the front steps. One of them carried a big yellow bag. They put on latex gloves and one took the professor's blood pressure and listened to his heart while another strapped a brace on his neck and bandaged his head wound.

"Do you know what happened?" The EMT asked.

Mrs. Morrison shook her head. "Not yet. There seems to have been a robbery."

"There was," Sally broke in. "That's what he whispered. 'Everything is gone'."

They all looked at the professor, who now seemed either deeply asleep or unconscious, and the paramedic stood up.

"We need to move him out," he said. "The police will be here soon, and you can tell them whatever you know.

"Where are you taking him?" Mrs. Morrison asked.

"Medical College Hospital," the paramedic said, and seconds later they were out the door, loading the professor in the ambulance, its red lights twirling on its roof as they got in and it slowly moved away, picking up speed, its sirens screaming until it vanished in the distance.

Mrs. Morrison took a deep breath. "Now tell me what's going on." She looked at Henry.

"I was showing Sally and Andrew some of my gardens," he began, "because Dad thought we might put our businesses together."

She nodded. "He told me."

Sally caught Andrew's eye. Thank goodness Henry was leaving out the part about the pull toy.

"When I knocked on the professor's door, it swung open," Henry went on, "so we came in. We thought something was wrong."

"Thank goodness you did," his mother said. "Heaven knows how long the poor man was lying here. Do you know if he has any family?"

Henry shook his head. "None I've seen."

"Never mind," Mrs. Morrison said. "The police can get that information." She turned as a car pulled up. "Here they are."

Three officers got out of the squad car – Lieutenant Miller and two others.

When they came in Lieutenant Miller glanced at Sally and Andrew. He looked surprised.

"We're friends with Henry," Andrew said quickly.

The Lieutenant looked at Mrs. Morrison. "Do you mind if we ask these children some questions?"

"Go ahead," she said. "They've done a very good job so far."

The Lieutenant asked why they were in the house, how they got in, what they saw first, what they saw next, and if they'd touched anything. His sergeant took notes, and two more policemen in dark blue jumpsuits came in and began dusting for fingerprints and taking pictures.

"I think that's everything," the Lieutenant finally said. "We'll call if we need more."

Andrew stood up straight. "And if we think of anything we forgot, we'll call you to report." He said in his police show voice.

They all heard a familiar voice as Henry's dad walked in, shaking hands with everyone. "How can I help?"

"Things are under control," Lieutenant Miller said. "I think we can overlook any breaking and entering charges, as the door was open and the children felt something was wrong. In fact, they did exactly what they should have, once they came in."

"Good." Mr. Morrison nodded. "Do you have any ideas about what happened?"

"We know there was a serious assault," Miller said. "According to the EMT's report, blunt trauma to the head. And we've heard from Sally," he gestured at her, "that some sort of robbery took place."

"Can you tell me what your technicians found?" Mr. Morrison asked.

Lieutenant Miller straightened his shoulders. "So far, given the open door with no forced entry marks, the victim answered his door because he was expecting someone. He probably knew his attacker. We sent a forensics team to the hospital to take his fingerprints. They're on the way here to compare them with what my techs have lifted."

"Anything else?" Mr. Morrison asked.

Miller looked at the officer standing behind him, who pulled out a notebook and started reading from it. "Footprint smudges, lots of fingerprints, looks like they were in the basement and came up carrying something out. It's a dirt floor and forensics says some things were moved, probably boxes. Whatever they were, they're gone, so that may be what they were after. No way to tell yet."

Lieutenant Miller's phone rang and he listened.

"The hospital," he punched off. "The professor has some swelling on his brain. He's been taken into surgery."

Mrs. Morrison made a small noise. "That's serious," she said. "And terrible."

"So it will be several days before you'll be allowed to interview him," Mr. Morrison added.

"I'm afraid so," Lieutenant Miller said.

"Mr. Morrison nodded. "All right. We'll let you get on with your work. I expect you'll be in touch."

"Yes, sir," the Lieutenant said. "Just as soon as we have more information."

Outside, Henry looked at his father. "Dad? I wasn't finished here at the professor's. In the garden, I mean."

"All right, but don't forget about your other jobs. And don't get in the way of the police. You'll need their permission to be in the garden."

Henry nodded.

"We can stay and help him," Andrew offered. "And check out how he works."

Mr. and Mrs. Morrison both smiled. "Our house is close by," Henry's mother said. "So come back with Henry later if you need a place to cool off, or some lemonade."

Sally smiled her thanks, but once Henry's parents had left, Andrew held up his hand before Henry could move. "We need to show you something," he said. "Where's your phone?" Henry handed it to Andrew who pulled up the Wikipedia article about the professor before he gave the phone back to Henry.

They watched Henry as he read it, slowly and carefully, his forehead crinkling.

Finally, he shoved his phone back in his pocket and sank down on the front steps. "You're right," he said, sounding sad. "This is my professor. His picture's with the article. I didn't know anything about his wooden toys idea."

Sally felt she knew what Henry was thinking. That someone he admired so much might be a criminal. She sat down beside him. "If we can get back on the porch to look for your cap, or even just get in the garden, there might be something those guys left behind," she said. "It's worth a try."

Henry stood up. "Okay. Let's do it."

They came up the alley and saw one of the policemen standing by the professor's back gate. He recognized them. "I hear you kids did a good job," he said, smiling.

"Thanks." Henry explained about leaving his cap, and when the officer started to shake his head Henry added, "I only need to look on the porch."

"Well..." the policeman looked doubtful. "I guess I can let you in. They've already gone over the ground out here. But not all three of you."

Sally gave him her best smile. "I'll wait here," she said.

"And don't disturb anything," the policeman added as the boys ran through the gate.

On the porch the piles of plastic mulch bags were

scattered, as though someone had gone through them. A quick look told Henry and Andrew there was no wooden pull toy lying underneath, and no sign of Henry's cap. They looked under the steps and under the porch and circled slowly around the garden.

"I guess it's gone," Henry whispered.

"And nothing else is here either." Andrew said.

They thanked the policeman and watched him walk back inside the gate as they came out. They were on their bikes when Andrew jumped back off. He took a few steps and reached down into a patch of scraggly grass beside the fence. His hand came up holding a piece of yellow paper.

"What?" Henry said.

"Some kind of sales ticket," Andrew said. "It looks new."

They peered over his shoulder.

"It's for a motorcycle tire," Sally said. "The date's from three days ago! Whoever was here has a motorcycle."

Andrew was peering down at the patch of grass. "Isn't that a tire track?"

"Looks like it," Henry said. "But they might not have had anything to do with the robbery. This grass is pretty far from the professor's gate." He took the ticket from Andrew. "And it says the store's in Midlothian, way across the river."

"So what?" Andrew said, "We know they were using motorcycles, so it could definitely be them." He took the ticket back and swung his leg over his bike seat. "I don't care how far away that store is," he said. "I'm going to find it. And when I get there, I'm going to find out who bought that tire and find him too."

CHAPTER SIX

Andrew had reached the end of the alley before Sally caught up with him, almost crashing when she swerved her bike across his path.

"What're you doing?" Andrew yelled. "Move!"

"You have to stop," she panted, bracing her front tire against his wheel.

"No I don't," he said, shoving at her handlebars. "Get out of my way. You're wasting time."

"Listen, Andrew. Remember when the police found a motorcycle tire print at the museum, and you said, that's our guy?"

"Of course I remember," Andrew said, backing up. "The guy with the headlamp and crowbar. The one who freaked you out. That's why I'm going."

Henry pulled up alongside him. "Wait. Hang on. Before you go flying off like that," he said, "you should be sure this tire is the same as the track they found at the museum. Otherwise you're wasting time."

"And the only way to find out is tell the police," Sally said. "They can take an imprint."

Andrew was still moving. "That'll take too long. You know we need to hurry. If this is our guy someone at this shop might know him and could tell us where he lives."

"And then what're you going to do?" Henry said. "Go to his house and arrest him, by yourself?"

Andrew's face turned red, and he gripped his handlebars. "No, but I can see if they're all there, or follow them if they start leaving...or maybe call 911...I'll figure it out, okay?" he said.

Sally looked at him, and felt a burst of affection for her brother, sitting there on his bike with sweat soaking his T-shirt and a stubborn look on his face. "Henry's right, Andrew. I know we wanted to do this by ourselves, but we can't. We've got to tell Mom."

There was a silence while Andrew stared at the ground. A dog barked in a yard further down the alley, but otherwise it was very quiet. Standing in the sun, Sally felt sweat trickling down her back. Then, slowly, Andrew looked up.

"Okay," he said, "I'll go show it to her."

"My house is closer than the Museum." Henry moved his bike aside. "My mom could call that police officer who was here."

"Thanks, but I found the ticket." Andrew started moving again, as Sally backed her bike away from his front wheel.

"We'll come with you," she said. "It'd be better if we're all there to explain."

She saw Henry's face tighten. "Not me," he said. "My mom thinks we're going to my house. She's probably made sandwiches and stuff."

"I'll come to your house, then," Sally said. This was not the time to hurt Henry's feelings. "Then I'll walk dogs and meet you at home," she said to Andrew.

Henry pointed at the yellow sales slip, still in Andrew's hand. "Be careful how you hold that. Think fingerprints."

Andrew's face reddened, and Sally knew he was embarrassed he hadn't thought of that himself. Without another word he rode out of the alley, speeding down the hill to Shockoe Slip, thinking hard while he was churning up the incline to Broad Street. This sales slip was real, and finding it made everything about the robbery seem more real too. He knew he'd have made a plan if he'd gone over to Midlothian, but it couldn't hurt to try Mom first, and let her tell the police. Every minute counted, before the people who had the toys did something horrible, like sell them all. Pedaling fast, he reached the Boulevard and the museum's parking lot and walked into his mother's office.

Surprised, his mother looked up from her laptop. Four tin toys sat beside it on her desk. "Andrew!" She sounded happy to see him. "Good! I was just cataloguing these toys. They're…"

"Mom, I've got something to tell you."

"I know about your finding that poor professor," she said. "A police officer called."

"Right," said Andrew. "But now there's more."

She sat back, listening closely, while Andrew told her about seeing the motorcycle guy with the crowbar, his and Sally's vow on the night of the robbery to get the toys back, and Henry's telling them that he might have seen a pull toy on a customer's porch. And their deciding to google antique wooden toys and finding a professor who talked about toys from the time of the American Revolution.

"It turned out that same guy lives in Henry's neighborhood, and he's one of Henry's best customers." Andrew finished. "So we went there this morning to find that pull toy. But it was gone, and then we found the professor, and after the police left we went back to look for it and that's when we found this sales ticket for a motorcycle tire and saw a tire print under it. We thought it might be the same motorcycle that was here at the museum." It all came out in a rush, and he realized his mother was staring at him. "We just wanted to help," he finished, thrusting his hand out with the ticket in it.

She was still silent, still looking at him. Finally she smiled. "Thank you," she said, getting up and coming around the desk. "I'll call Lieutenant Miller right now."

Andrew let out his breath and shoved his hair back from his forehead. "My fingerprints are on the ticket, but only where I held it."

"I'm sure the police can deal with that," his mother said as she dialed.

In a minute she was peering at the sales slip Andrew held and reading the tire's make and number to the Lieutenant. "Of course. I'm in my office," she said and hung up. "He's sending an officer to get it right now."

Minutes later a policeman strode in and shook hands with both of them. "Officer Knudsen," he said.

"I remember you," Andrew said. "From the night of the robbery."

"I remember you too," Officer Knudsen said, turning to Mom. "The Lieutenant gave me the information you called in. We're checking the specs and tread now, and if you'll show me what you've found…"

Mom pointed to her desk and the officer used large tweezers to carefully pick up the ticket and read it carefully. "Whoever bought this tire paid cash, but the clerk might have known him, or be able to give us a description. So, if it's the same tire, we might have our first real break." He turned to Andrew. "Nice work," he said.

Andrew felt a rush of pleasure, which faded as Lieutenant Knudsen went on. "However, we still don't know who we're dealing with. They could be amateurs, or seasoned criminals, really bad guys. Considering what happened to the professor, I'm leaning toward really bad." He paused, then spoke very slowly. "So, I need to repeat what I told you on the night of the robbery: we want you to stay away from this case. It's bad enough to have the toys missing and the professor hurt. We don't need any more problems."

Andrew's face turned red. "I just wanted to help my mom," he said.

"So do we all," the policeman said. And then unexpectedly, he smiled. "And now, thanks to you, we stand a better chance." He turned to Mrs. Corbett. "I'll be in touch when I have news."

"Thank you," she smiled at him. "Fingers crossed."

After Officer Knudsen left, Mom gave Andrew a big hug. "You've really, really, helped," she said. "But I love you, and I don't want you in danger, okay?"

"Okay," Andrew muttered, feeling like a little kid.

"Now let's both get back to work and meet at noon. At home," Mom said. "By then we might know something."

But at lunchtime, when Andrew hurried into the kitchen hoping for news, his mother shook her head.

"Nothing yet," she said, "But I'm sure we'll hear soon. You gave the police something real to look for."

Mac had made tomato and Smithfield ham sandwiches slathered with mayonnaise, and left sliced cucumbers in a bowl beside a dish of raw carrots. Sally and Jane were already eating, and they jumped when Mom's phone rang. Her hands full, she nodded to Andrew, who grabbed it from her handbag.

"This is Andrew Corbett," he said trying to make his voice sound deeper. "Yes, sir." He listened. "So the sales ticket's definitely for the same tire as the one at the museum? Wow! Cool!" He listened some more. "Yes sir, okay. Tomorrow night. Thanks, I'll tell my Mom." He hung up and turned around.

"They found the store!" He blurted out. "And the owner remembers the sale because his clerk spent so much time talking to the guy who bought the tire. The police can't question the clerk today – he left yesterday for a three-day fishing trip and he's not answering his phone. The police went to his house and his mother backed up his fishing story, so they have to wait 'til he gets back tomorrow night. Which is too long to wait," he added under his breath.

"Couldn't they look where he keeps his boat?" Sally asked.

"All his mother could tell the police was he usually goes to the Chesapeake Bay. She doesn't know exactly where." Andrew said.

Mom looked thoughtful. "That's something, anyway." She started to say more, but Jane stood up.

"Can I work for Andrew this afternoon? I can do my homework after supper."

Mom nodded, and Andrew turned to Sally. "Let's go."

They walked outside into a blast of mid-day heat, so thick and steamy it felt almost as if they needed to push it away. "Whew!" Mom said, coming down the steps. "We're getting thunderstorms later. A big storm cell, the weather says. Watch out for lightning, please."

Andrew looked at the sky as they hopped on their bikes, and at Mr. Kelso's, he led them straight inside the coop. "You two can let the birds out and clean the coop," he said. "When you finish, rattle the feed tray the way I showed you, and they'll come in."

Jane looked pleased, but Sally frowned. "You're doing something else?"

"If I ride fast, I can make it to Midlothian before the storm comes," Andrew said, not meeting her eyes.

"What about what Officer Knudsen said?" Sally said, walking closer. "And how do you think Mom'll feel if she finds out you totally ignored what he told you?"

"She'd get really upset," Andrew admitted. "But she'll be a lot more upset if she loses her job. We all will!" Andrew turned and started walking out of the coop. "That clerk might not be fishing at all, and if whoever stole the toys are using these two days to leave town with them, we're sunk. I'm going."

Suddenly, Jane ran at Andrew and punched his back with her small fist, her eyes filling with tears.

"Sally's right, you shouldn't go," she wailed, blinking hard. "Something bad could happen. Like it did with Dad."

Andrew turned around. "So what am I supposed to do?" he said, his voice tight. He swallowed and rubbed his back where Jane had hit him. "Just let those guys get away?"

For a minute no one moved, then Sally held up her hands. "No, we can't let them get away," she said. "But you're not going to Midlothian. I am."

Andrew started to shake his head, but Sally stopped

him. "I'm older than you, and I didn't promise anyone anything."

Andrew didn't move, and she thought he was still going to argue. But instead he pulled his phone from the pocket of his shorts and clicked on a map. "Okay. Here're some short cuts to the tire store."

They bent over the screen, spotting the back roads that had less traffic. Then Sally put on her helmet. "What am I supposed to do when I get there?" She said.

"Ask for that clerk, maybe pretend you know him. Like where's his house, stuff like that." Andrew said. "If he's not really fishing you might be able to find him."

"Okay. I'll be back as soon as I can."

She walked her bike out of Mr. Kelso's gate and hopped on when she bumped off the curb. Past the museum the boulevard went west before it wound through a big park scattered with magnolia trees, their white blossoms sending a sweet scent across the hot breeze. She reached the big bridge that crossed the river and coasted down to the narrow pedestrian sidewalk, where she got off and walked beside the rushing cars. Below her the broad, muddy river swirled around big rocks and tiny tree-covered islands, and she could see people wading or sitting on the rocks with their feet in the water. She almost relaxed until she looked up at the sky and saw clouds starting to pile up in the west. They were still far off and not yet black, but dark enough to make her hesitate, one foot still on the sidewalk. Then she shook her head. Andrew was right. They didn't have much time. She couldn't go back, no matter what kind of storm was coming.

Suddenly a picture of Zorro flashed through her mind. What would he do if he were here? Maybe he'd lift her up behind him in the saddle and gallop straight to the tire store. She giggled, wondering what the people in the cars would think as she and Zorro flashed by. But then she had another, surprising, thought – she didn't really need Zorro. She was doing the same thing he would, only on her bike instead of a horse. She just needed to ride faster.

She jumped back on and speeded to the end of the bridge, looking on her phone, she saw the next road on the map. It was narrow and winding, following the river under a tunnel of deep green trees. A damp breeze was coming across the river, bringing a smell she loved...dark soil, wet grass and water, all mixed together.

Under the trees she pedaled even faster, stealing quick glances at the river flowing close beside the road. It moved lazily, wide and flat, with sandbars where she saw big gray herons standing in the shallows. From the corner of her eye she saw one of them suddenly plunge its long beak into the water and spear a fish. She winced at the way the heron swallowed the fish before he went flapping away up the river through the sunlight, long legs dangling. Then she made herself concentrate on pedaling, and she started chanting, "I'm getting there, I'm getting there, I can do it," in time with the whirring sound of her pedals.

In a few minutes she saw a narrow road winding up a hill, too steep to pedal up. Pushing her bike, she saw dark clouds all across the sky to the west. And then thunder rumbled, low and ominous.

Breathless, she hopped back on and pedaled with one eye on the sky and the other on the road, and ten minutes later she rounded a wide curve. There, down the hill and a short distance ahead, stood a building with a large sign painted on its roof. The sign said "MOTORCYCLES." She braked, wiped her face with her sleeve, and took a swig of water. Then she coasted smoothly down the hill and into the tire store's parking lot.

She propped her bike next to the building's stucco front and pushed through the glass door, almost falling over a row of motorcycles standing on the floor in front of her. All kinds of tires were piled behind them. At first she thought no one was in the store, but then she saw a man in the back, bending over behind a counter. He straightened up and smiled at her.

"Can I help?" He asked.

"I, uh, yes," Sally stammered, suddenly nervous. "I, uh, I'm looking for a friend…a friend of my brother's." It came out in a rush. "He works here. He was fixing a tire for my brother's bike, and my brother sent me to get it."

"What kind of tire?" The man asked. "Do you know the brand?"

Sally thought fast. "My brother didn't tell me," she answered. "But his friend knows."

"You're probably talking about my clerk, Jason," the man said. "He's not here. He asked for a couple of days off."

"Oh, no," Sally moaned. "My brother will be so mad at me." She looked at the man hopefully. "Do you know where he went?"

The storekeeper looked at her curiously. "Fishing," he answered. "I'm sorry." He started to turn away, and without stopping to think, Sally touched his arm. "Do you think I could go to his house?" She said. "I mean, in case he comes back early?"

The storekeeper turned around. "You must have a mean brother," he said. "You sound pretty desperate."

"I am," Sally said, edging around some tires.

"Well, he does live near here," the man said. "I suppose it would be all right." But then he frowned. "Wait a minute. The police were here this noon, asking about a tire. A motorcycle tire. And about my clerk, Jason."

"But mine's a bicycle tire," she said quickly, seeing the storekeeper shaking his head. Finally he said, "Well, you look pretty harmless. I'll write the address for you."

A bell tinkled over the front door and a tall man walked in, a long ponytail under his baseball cap.

"I'm in a hurry," he called in a loud, gruff voice. "I ordered a new tire for my truck, and I need to pick it up now. There's a bad storm coming." He brushed past Sally as if she was invisible.

"I'll be right with you," the storekeeper told him, busy writing on a piece of paper.

"I haven't got all day," the man said, walking to the back of the store to inspect a shiny red motorcycle.

Sally's felt the goose bumps on her neck and arms first. Then her stomach lurched. She knew where she'd heard that voice before…at the museum! The blind man, shouting at Andrew! And he was here, without his dark glasses and cane! His voice was unmistakable, and his long blond ponytail clinched it. She lowered her head and turned sideways, hoping he wouldn't notice her.

"Do you live around here?" It took Sally a few seconds to realize the storekeeper was talking to her.

"Uh…" Sally tried to stop panicking, "Uh…," she repeated, trying to think. "We used to," she fibbed, "but I don't remember all the streets."

The storekeeper nodded, still writing on the paper. "If Jason's back early, tell him I want to talk to him." He handed her the little map he'd drawn with a street number. "Here's where you go. You won't have any trouble finding it. He lives with his mother."

Thank you." Sally managed to say, still keeping her head turned sideways.

And without another word, she sprinted to the door.

CHAPTER SEVEN

Outside, large silver raindrops were beginning to splatter the parking lot's asphalt. Sally raced to her bike and hopped on, tangling one foot in her spokes. She risked a quick look behind as she sped away, but the man hadn't followed her.

The big drops were turning into real rain as she put several blocks behind her, but she pulled over and sat for a minute, ignoring getting soaked. The man in the baseball cap had pretended to be blind when he was at the museum's storeroom. Now he was at the same store where someone with a motorcycle had bought a tire, which had left a print by the museum. There has to be a connection, she thought. But what?

She knew she had to move, but what should she do? The rain was turning into a solid downpour, and if she called Andrew now her phone would get soaked. She'd better get to the clerk's house first. She looked at the small map the storekeeper had given her, trying to keep it covered with her hand while her hair grew plastered to her face. She heard a rumble of thunder, then a loud crack overhead, so loud she jumped and almost fell off her bike. The map showed a right turn at the next street and she headed for that, avoiding the flooding gutters and big puddles and ducking at the almost constant flashes of lightning, but pedaling more slowly as she looked for the house number.

Finally she saw it, on a mailbox in front of a dirt driveway. The driveway was awash with rivulets and lined with thick bushes, but it led to a yard and a house with a small front porch. She was halfway to the house when a white-hot streak of lightning split the sky with such a terrifying, sizzling BANG that she hurled her bike into the bushes and threw herself on the ground underneath.

"Wow!" she gasped. "That was really close."

She wiped dirt off her nose and mouth and started to get up when there was another flash of light behind her. Something with headlights had turned into the driveway. Sally scuttled backward and saw a white van heading straight for the yard, going fast. It skidded to a stop in front of the porch, splattering mud in every direction and braking so hard one of the dented doors at its rear came open. The driver's door flew open as well, and a young man with red hair jumped out and raced up the steps into the house.

Sally's heart pounded. "It's him," she whispered. "It's got to be. Now what do I do?"

Sally would never be able to explain what she did next. Rising to her feet, she lowered her head against the pelting rain and ran straight to the back of the van. She grabbed the open door's handle, pulled herself up, and hopped inside. The door flew out again in the wind, but she grabbed its inside handle and slammed it shut. There were no rear seats, only a pile of fishing nets on the floor, and Sally flung herself down and slid under them just as the house door banged again. She heard the man's voice call out something about being home in a few days, and before she could breathe he jumped in and started the engine. She could feel the wheels spin, then the van was splattering down the driveway, then it swerved onto the street. She was trapped.

"I've got to get out," she whispered aloud.

But she knew it was too late. The driver was going too fast. She'd have to wait 'til he slowed down somewhere. Pulling the nets with her, she slithered closer to the back doors to be ready. At least the two front seats had high headrests that would make it hard for him to see in the back through the rearview mirror. The rain was coming down in torrents, thudding like drumbeats on the van's roof, so loud she could hardly think. But it made the driver slow to a crawl while he peered through the windshield, trying to see past the flailing wipers.

Sally wormed closer to the door, pushing back on the nets. Just a tiny bit slower, she thought as she put her hand on the door handle. But suddenly she had another thought. *If he hadn't been fishing, where had he been? And where was he going now? Probably to wherever the robbers had hidden the toys.* I've got to stay, she thought.

She pushed herself back under the nets, making as

small a hump as she could, and huddled down to wait. She needed to text Andrew, but if she told him she was in the back of a van speeding through the storm with no idea where she was going, there was nothing he could do. Better to wait.

And the van was speeding up again, no longer turning corners. They must be on a straight road somewhere, probably leaving town. She could use her phone's GPS, she thought, and try to figure out where they were. She was easing it out of her shorts' pocket when the van swerved, hard. Through the back windows she could see trees, lots of them. She could hear them hitting the sides of the van and heavy branches brushing across the roof. They must be on a very narrow road, and from the way the van was bouncing, probably dirt. They swerved hard again, and the man suddenly slammed on the brakes and skidded to a stop, just the way he had at the other house. Before she could move, he'd thrown open his door, jumped out and banged it shut behind him.

Sally froze. Wait. Just wait, she thought. If he's gone I can jump out too. If he hasn't...

She let out her breath. Nothing. Not a sound. She counted to ten, and then slowly raised her head to peer to the front 'til she could see through the windshield. Through the pouring rain she could dimly make out a small building. It was a shack – no, it was made of logs – it was a cabin. Its front door was close to the front of the van, but its one small window was further along the wall and had shutters that were closed.

Slowly, Sally reached for the back door handle and pushed. It opened a crack. Nothing. She pushed it further. The rain was coming down harder than ever, but she could see a wall of trees straight in front of her, about twenty feet away. She slid through the opening, felt her feet on the ground and stood up, shutting the door behind her. Thunder was rumbling and banging so loudly she couldn't hear anything. Cautiously she peered around the van's back corner.

No one was there.

"Okay," she whispered, "Go for it."

She took one more deep breath and crossed her fingers, and then, keeping the van between herself and the cabin, she bolted into the trees.

"The police told my mom I couldn't do any more investigating," Andrew said. "So Sally went."

"But has she called or anything?" Henry asked, wiping rain off his face. He had arrived at Mr. Kelso's to find Andrew and Jane sitting on bird crates in the shed, waiting out the storm.

"Only a text when she got to the tire store," Andrew answered. "I texted her back twice, but she hasn't answered."

Henry frowned. "I'll try my phone." After a minute

he looked up. "Nothing. Maybe it's the lightning." He frowned again. "So, I think one of us has to go out there. And since you can't, that means me."

"Go where?" Andrew said. "The tire store?"

"That's the best place to start, isn't it?" Henry got up and peered out the door. "And I should go now. This storm's got to stop some time."

"Okay," Andrew said. "But hurry. If we go home Mac will start asking questions."

Henry nodded. "I'll text you as soon as I know something. And text me if she calls."

He walked his bike through big puddles 'til he could hop on outside the gate. At the other side of the long bridge his phone beeped. "Sally?" He said.

Her voice was faint. "I just got reception."

"Where are you?" Henry said.

"On a road outside Midlothian. I've done something crazy. And I don't have my bike."

"Okay, hang on..." Henry's fingers were sliding fast across his screen, "... yeah, I see you. Stay there. I'm on my way."

He rode fast on the tree-lined road, through the village and out again on another straight road until he saw her waving. He braked hard, his tires squealing on the wet surface. "Are you okay?" he said.

"Yes." She sounded excited.

"OK. My phone's good. I'll text Andrew." Henry put down his kickstand and got off, hearing a cow mooing in a field across the road. "So what's going on?"

"This," she said, showing him her phone. On it was a picture of a huge tree, its trunk split wide open, lying across the driveway of a small cabin.

Henry whistled. "Big!" He said.

"It got hit by lightning," Sally said, "And I was really close. But it's the cabin I'm showing you. I found the clerk, and he's in that cabin."

Henry stared at her. "Wonder Woman!" He said admiringly.

She *had* been gutsy, Sally thought, surprised at how pleased his words made her feel. "And we've got to get back there," she said. "I'm sure the toys are inside."

But Henry was shaking his head. "Not until I hear the rest," he said, leading the way into trees that partly sheltered them from the rain.

She told him, starting with the blind guy in the museum yesterday morning, the same man in the tire store today, except this time without the cane and dark glasses. "He's definitely not blind," she said, "he was just pretending yesterday at the museum."

Henry looked thoughtful. "He could have come back to snoop around and find out how much the police know. And he could have gone to the store to meet up with that clerk, Jason. His truck's tire could have been an excuse."

"Maybe," Sally said, "But that cabin's a perfect hiding place. And with your bike we can get there fast."

Henry glanced at the sky, seeing no chance of the

rain stopping. "You're right, the toys could be there. But they might not be, either. And even if they are, there's no way for him to get that tree cut up and off that dirt road tonight. You said yourself it's flooded. And he couldn't walk out carrying all the boxes; it's too far from town. So he's stuck, at least for tonight."

"If you don't want to, I'll go by myself." Sally said, a stubborn look on her face.

Henry held up his hand. "With only one bike to get away? And it'll be dark soon?"

She was quiet. "Then maybe we should tell our parents, and they can go?"

Henry's head turned. "Are you serious? Tell them you found a guy the police have a huge manhunt out for, you got in his van, he drove to a cabin out in the middle of nowhere, and you barely had time to jump out before he saw you?" He raised his eyebrows at her. "And didn't the police tell you and Andrew to stay out of it?" He walked over to his bike, "If they rush all the way out here and the toys aren't there…"

"They'll be totally furious," she finished for him. "Okay. So what do we do?"

"Come back in the morning," he said. "With Andrew. And, if we actually find the toys, call our parents and they can tell the police. Then they might forget that all along we've been doing exactly what they told us not to do."

Sally took a deep breath. Much as she hated to admit it, he was right. "Really early, then," she said.

He nodded and pushed his bike toward her. "Ride this. I'll run." He got out his phone. "What's the name of the street you left your bike on?"

She told him, holding the handlebars while he looked at his phone's screen.

After he stuffed it back in his pocket she climbed on his bike. Somehow she knew he was being this cautious because he wanted to find the toys just as much as she and Andrew did, and if anything went wrong it could be their fault. Why hadn't she believed that sooner? Probably because they didn't know each other very well. Now, each thing was helping them know each other better, and she was liking the person she was getting to know.

Her bike was where she'd left it, lying on its side in the bushes beside Jason's driveway. Other than a light in one window, the house was quiet. She wheeled her bike to the street and they took off again, riding side by side. The only sounds were the falling rain and their pedals turning rapidly, almost in rhythm. When they came to the end of the long bridge, Henry pulled over.

"So meet here? 7:30?" He said.

She nodded. "Be on time."

Andrew met her in the front hall, looking upset. "You could have texted more," he said.

"No I couldn't. Too much happened." She walked

through the house toward the kitchen, but then she kept going into the garden. "We need to be out here so no one can hear me," she said. "I have a ton to tell you."

When she'd finished Andrew looked stunned, but then his face split into a wide smile. "Wow," he said after a minute, "Are you sure you can find the cabin again?"

Sally nodded. "I know I can. And we've got to get up really early."

"Right." Andrew started pacing, thinking. "I knew something was up with that blind man. Remember he was wearing a watch? He's mixed up in this somehow. I know it."

"Maybe," Sally said. "He's really weird, anyway."

She heard a hiccup and turned around. Jane was holding a Lego spaceship, her mouth quivering. "I asked Andrew to help me," she said to Sally, "but all he did was walk around looking at his phone."

"He was worried about me." Sally gave her a quick hug.

"And I heard what you said about going to a cabin tomorrow," Jane said. "So I'm going too. You know I can ride my bike really fast."

Andrew turned on her, his tone angry. "No, you're not. You have to act like nothing's going on. And you can't, I repeat, CAN'T, tell anybody about the cabin or anything else you just heard."

Jane's small chin stuck out, and her face started to pucker.

"You know you have to go to school," Sally said. "But you can help us a lot if you'll do what Andrew told you, and not say anything. Can you remember that?"

Jane nodded, still sniffling. "Of course I can," she said. "I'm not that little."

"Good," Sally said. "I'll take you next time, I promise."

"So what time did Henry say?" Andrew asked, looking at his phone. "Hold on, this is him." Reading, he frowned. "Bad news. The professor's awake and wants to see him. His mom's taking him in the morning, and he's asking if we'll be okay if we go by ourselves." He looked at Sally. "There's no way we're waiting," he said.

"Of course we're not," Sally said. "We can't let that guy get away."

CHAPTER EIGHT

"I hear you're the brave soul who rescued me," Professor Saunders said.

"Me and my friends," Henry answered, startled at how pale the professor looked, propped up in his hospital bed. An IV was taped to his arm.

The professor gestured at the two chairs in his room. "Please, sit down," he said. "I want to explain."

Henry and Mrs. Morrison sat, and the professor leaned back against his pillow.

"Sir, I saw you online," Henry said. "You said the guys who started this country – you call them the Founding Fathers – had to meet in secret because the British were trying to catch them. When they sent each other messages, sometimes they hid them in their kids' toys."

The professor smiled. "You learned my theory." Then he sighed and stared into space. "But you don't know how hard it's been to prove. People who own old toys don't want them pried open, especially by some crazy professor with a crazy theory. Although," he sat up straighter, his voice firm, "It's not so crazy. I've done the research."

He looked around the room, but Henry could tell

he wasn't seeing the TV in the corner or the hospital's helicopter pad outside the window. He was miles away in another world, the world of history he loved. Henry shifted in his chair, and the professor started talking again.

"Last year," he said, "one of my graduate students heard about the toy exhibit coming to the museum. That student knows my theory, and said he knew a staff member who might let us borrow a few toys for a day. I became so excited, I lost my common sense and didn't ask any questions. Considering what happened, I should have." He stopped to sip some water and took several deep breaths.

"Are you sure you want to talk this much now?" Mrs. Morrison looked worried. "We can come back later."

The professor shook his head. "I'm fine." He put down the glass and leaned back. "I never dreamed my student, Jason, was going to rob the museum. He was my top scholar." The professor sounded proud. "Always buried in a book and a little naive, but a fine young man."

Mrs. Morrison leaned forward, "Maybe you inspired him, so he was willing to do anything to help you."

"And maybe he wanted to prove your theory too," Henry added.

The professor stared at them. "Those are lovely ideas. But they don't change what happened."

"So what did happen?" Henry tried not to sound impatient, but he couldn't help wondering what Sally and

Andrew were doing. The professor must have noticed because he hurried on. "The night of the robbery, Jason called to tell me he had to work — he's a clerk in a tire store — but two of his friends would bring the toys to my house."

Henry nearly jumped from his chair. The tire store! So it *was* the right place! And this guy Jason probably was the clerk the owner had told Sally about!

"Shortly afterwards two men arrived at my door," the professor continued. "They brought several boxes in, put them in my basement, and asked me to pay them for their delivery services. Jason hadn't said anything about money — but I paid them, of course. Even then I didn't realize anything was wrong."

He stopped to sip more water. "I did wonder why there was more than one box, but I was too excited to give that much thought. I went to bed, eager to start work the next morning. Jason had promised to come, but when he didn't appear I opened the box on top and took the pull toy to the back porch." The professor glanced at Henry. "The one you saw when you came that afternoon."

Henry nodded.

"After you left I began trying to open it. I had to go very, very slowly, and be very, very careful. Finally, knowing I had one more day before the toys would have to go back, I decided to stop and wait for Jason." His voice slowed, his eyes closing as though he was seeing something he didn't want to see.

"After I'd gone to bed that night, a loud bump woke me up. I went to the top of the stairs to listen, but I didn't hear anything more. I went downstairs, just in case, and I could see the front door was open. I walked forward..." he stopped talking, looking sad. "That's all I remember."

"That's when they knocked you out," Henry finished for him, and the professor nodded.

"I'm very thankful you found me, or I might not be here in this hospital bed," he said.

"Me too." Henry smiled.

They were interrupted by a loud knock on the door. A nurse came in and wheeled her cart up to the professor's bed. They watched her put a thermometer in the professor's mouth and take his blood pressure.

When she left the professor asked, "Do the police have any new leads?"

"Nothing we've heard this morning," Mrs. Morrison answered, standing up. "But they're working hard."

Henry, feeling terrible about how sad the professor looked, stood up too. For a minute he desperately wanted to tell the professor and his mom everything he knew. But his mother was moving to the door. "Now you really do need to rest," she said to the professor. "But we'll come back soon."

"Thank you," the professor called after them. "I'd like that."

Walking down the hall Henry was silent. At the elevator his mother turned to look at him. "Penny for your thoughts," she said.

He jumped, then swallowed. "I feel so bad for the professor," he said. "I hope that student'll go to jail when they find him."

"It doesn't sound like he meant any real harm, but he certainly let things get out of hand," she answered. "I'm sure his two friends will go to jail though, when the police catch them."

If they catch them, Henry thought. Or if we do.

"Shhh!" Sally hissed at Andrew. "He's right in front of us!"

Andrew froze, taking his weight off the branch that had just cracked. He was right behind Sally, pushing through the bushes alongside the dirt road that led to the cabin. But the young man standing in the muddy clearing didn't seem to hear. He was holding a chainsaw, his dark red hair glinting in the morning sun. The big tree lay in chunks on either side of the road between puddles of yesterday's rainwater.

Sally edged closer, and then she nodded to Andrew and stepped out into the road. Startled, the man whirled. "What do you want?" He called.

"We want to know where the toys are," Sally said in a loud voice. She saw him tense, but he didn't move. "What toys?" He said. "I don't know what you're talking

about!

"Yes, you do." Andrew moved up beside her. His voice was just as loud, and angry. "And we know your name is Jason. You work at the tire shop, and we know you took the toys. Professor Saunders told us."

Jason stared at him, and then at Sally again. "I'm busy," he said. "You should leave. Whatever you think you're doing, there's nothing here. So please go."

Sally held up her phone. "We're not going anywhere 'til you tell us where the toys are. I can send your picture to the police. They'll be happy to know where you are."

A long minute went by, all three of them standing still. Then Jason said quietly, "No, don't do that. But this is none of your business. You should stay out of it."

"It *is* our business." Andrew sounded as furious as he felt. "It's our mom's exhibit, and she'll lose her job if we don't get the toys back."

Jason sighed. He ran his hand through his hair, and Sally thought he seemed younger than he had at first.

"Okay," he said. "You're right, I was the professor's student, and I tried to get the museum staff to lend me a few toys. But they wouldn't, and I knew this would be the only chance the professor would have to test his theory. So I decided to borrow them on my own, just for a day or two. I was going to bring them right back without the professor's ever knowing what I'd done. I knew he wouldn't hurt them, and if he found a message it'd be huge." Jason shook his head. "So I got these two guys

I knew from the tire store to do it because they're great with electronics — alarms and stuff like that. I had no idea they'd take so many, and then go back to his house to steal them. I didn't know until my mom told me the police were looking for me, and I came out here to hide."

"Did your mom tell you the professor's in the hospital?" Sally said. "That they knocked him unconscious?"

Jason closed his eyes. "That's awful," he said in a low voice.

"So where've they gone?" Andrew interrupted. "We have to find them."

"I don't know," Jason said, shaking his head.

"I don't believe you," Andrew said, still sounding furious.

"They never answered me when I tried to get hold of them yesterday, and I have no idea where they are now. Or where the toys are either. I swear."

"So if you're telling the truth, you have to help us find them," Sally said. Jason stared at her, then at Andrew, who was still glaring at him. He looked off to the side for a minute. "I need to think," he said.

"You'd better think you're going to help," Sally said.

"Of course I'm going to help," Jason said firmly, surprising her. "I'm just not sure where to start."

"Maybe you didn't notice anything at the time," Andrew said, "but maybe they said something. Like, 'these toys must be worth a lot of money.'"

Sally looked at her brother. Cool, she thought.

Jason frowned. "Well, one of them, Ted, did say they'd be worth a lot up north, in Philadelphia or New York. Like 'I wonder how much these toys would go for in an antique store.' And the other guy, Mike, said 'a lot, I'll bet, if they weren't going back to that museum.'"

"And I bet they were thinking, 'Maybe we can steal them'," Andrew said.

Jason sighed. "Maybe. But that doesn't tell us where they are now."

"No," Andrew said slowly, "But they must have had a place to take them. Like wherever they live."

"Do you know where they live?" Sally asked.

"I might," Jason answered. "I was only at Ted's place once, down in the Fan District. But I think I can find it again."

"So if we load our bikes in your van," she said, "we can get there fast."

They hurried to pile everything in, and when Jason started the engine Sally looked back at the little cabin, standing forlornly in the sun. She'd been so sure the toys would be there, and now they'd wasted half a morning. Except it wasn't all wasted, she thought. Now they had help, and maybe that help could get them closer to finding the toys somewhere else.

On the main road Jason picked up speed, making Sally remember her wild ride yesterday and wonder how she'd ever had the nerve to jump inside. Zorro, she thought, I learned it from Zorro. She smiled and watched Andrew texting Henry where to meet them. "Better give him a heads up that Jason's on our side," she said in a low voice.

"We can't be totally sure yet," Andrew whispered back, but he looked less angry than he had, and they watched as Jason turned onto Laurel Street and drove slowly past a row of small, dilapidated-looking houses, all painted different colors.

He pointed at one in the middle of the block. "I think that's it," he said. "That greenish one. I'll park around the corner, just in case Ted's home. Don't want him to see my van, or me."

Henry rode up just as they climbed out of the van onto a shady sidewalk, and they followed Jason back around the corner and down the block to the green house. Jason went up the porch steps and rang the bell. While they waited Sally watched a sparrow hopping around on the grass, pecking for seeds. Every now and then it cheeped loudly, and Sally wondered if it had a nest of babies somewhere. Feeling hot, she pulled her hair onto the top of her head then the sound of voices made her look up. A grey-haired woman in a blue dress stood in the doorway of the house next door, a small dog jumping around her feet. It was too far away to hear what she was saying, but they could see her nodding her head before she closed the door.

"Found it!" Jason called as he came down the steps.

"Ted does live here. That woman thinks his friend's with him because she saw them both this morning. And, she heard them saying they were going to work."

"Did she know where they work?" Henry asked.

"No," Jason said, and Andrew groaned. "Great, now what?"

"Try another neighbor," Sally said. "Someone else might know."

Jason went to the house on the other side, but no one answered.

"We'll just have to wait," Henry said, looking around for some shade. "This house is all we've got."

"Okay." Andrew bumped his bike off the sidewalk. "Those guys'll probably be a while, so if I hurry I can go check on some of my clients' dogs that could be needing water. He looked at Sally. "It'll be quicker if you help."

"I'll stay here," Henry said. He didn't need to add that it was too soon to completely trust Jason.

"We'll be fast," Andrew called over his shoulder as he and Sally took off on their bikes, the sunlight reflecting off their helmets as they pedaled in and out of the trees' deep green shade. The first dog, a bull terrier, had knocked over his water bowl and was panting hard. Sally ran to fill it while Andrew jogged an Irish Setter around the block.

"We're lucky their owners'll be home after work," Andrew said. "And today's Mr. Kelso's half day. If I text him he'll do the pigeons himself."

Sally nodded. "Let's get some food before we go back. I'm starving."

"Okay. I just hope Mac doesn't ask a lot of questions."

But Mac was so busy fixing Jane's lunch that she barely looked up when they walked in the kitchen. Jane had Peaches on her lap while she munched a chicken sandwich, and Mac pointed to more sandwiches on a platter. Then she gave them a sharp glance while Andrew took one and ate it standing up.

"You two look like you've had a busy morning," Mac said.

"We have." Sally's throat felt tight, and her words came out in a squeak. She sat down and bit into an apple she'd taken from the fruit bowl.

"Lots of storm damage," Andrew added quickly.

"That bad?" Mac asked.

"Uh, nothing we can't fix," Andrew said, "But it'll take the rest of the day to clean up. We might be late getting home." He gulped down another sandwich while Mac told him to sit down and eat it slowly.

"Don't have time," Andrew said rummaging in the refrigerator.

"I'll be taking your sister swimming," Mac said. "So I'll see you tonight."

When she'd gone upstairs to collect her bathing suit, Andrew grabbed some slices of bread and cheese and put them in a bag. "We better hurry," he said. "Those guys could come back any time."

Then he realized Jane was staring at them. "What guys?" She said. "You and Sally are doing something again." Her voice quivered and she pushed Peaches off her lap. "I never said anything, so now you have to tell me. You promised."

Sally's heart gave a thump. She took a deep breath and made her voice sound level. "What we're doing is trying to help Mom," she said, feeling guilty. It wasn't a lie, but it wasn't the whole truth either.

"But why're you taking food?" Jane said.

"If we work late we might get hungry." Andrew looked at Sally. They heard Mac coming down the stairs, so Sally smiled at Jane and stood up.

"Your glasses really look good, you know. Just don't forget to take them off when you're swimming."

"Of course I won't, silly." Jane started to giggle. She wriggled down from her chair and picked Peaches up again. "But next time, you have to take me with you."

"Deal," Sally said. "Soon."

On the sidewalk Andrew stopped, looking at his phone. "It's from Henry," he said.

Sally put her foot on the curb and squinted at his screen. The text read: *Just found out where they work.*

CHAPTER NINE

"So where do they work?" Sally pushed her kickstand down beside Jason's van.

"At the police stables," Jason said. "The guy next door told us, but he didn't know which one. There're three of them. Stables, I mean."

"So how do we choose?" Andrew asked.

"Choose the closest," Henry said. "We looked it up, it's in Shockoe Slip. But we can't all go, we've got to watch this house too in case Ted and his friend come home." He looked at Jason. "I'm guessing it wouldn't be good if they saw you, so Andrew and I can go." He looked at Sally. "Okay with you?"

She nodded. "Sure." Actually it would be a relief not to have to ride all over the city during the hottest part of the day. And she'd have time to talk to Jason. She sat down next to him on the curb, the concrete hot under her shorts.

But Jason was looking worriedly at the boys. "Listen, guys, be really careful. Ted's not a nice guy. Don't let him see you."

"He doesn't even know us," Andrew said. "What's the big deal if he sees us?"

"Not in that neighborhood," Jason said. "It's all

ravines and vacant lots. Two guys riding nice bikes, he'll notice you."

"Whatever." Andrew's jaw tightened. "If anyone sees us, we'll just say we're looking at horses. Stop freaking out. We've got a plan."

"Actually," Henry broke in. "It's not a plan. We need to decide on a plan."

"Well, we don't have much to go on yet," Jason pointed out. "For now our plan could be that you two report what you see at the stables, and no one does anything until we all talk."

Henry and Sally nodded, while Andrew looked down at the sidewalk.

"Okay," Henry said. "So I know where Shockoe Slip is, but not the stables."

Jason's finger was sliding across his screen. "Here… take Cary Street down to Adams. Then go straight across town to Brook Road; it goes all the way to Shockoe Slip. The railroad tracks will be at the bottom, and you follow those southeast" – he was moving his finger over the map – "to here. Here're the stables."

"Got it," Andrew said in his TV police-show voice. "Let's go."

It was ten blocks down Cary Street to Adams, and at Adams they turned north and began riding straight across the city. Fewer trees lined these downtown streets and the afternoon sun blazed on their necks and arms. Finally Henry pulled up under a large maple tree, its shade covering a patch of cool damp earth. They eased off their bikes and unhooked their water bottles. Andrew wiped the sweat off his face with his sleeve. A picture of the quarry's cool, dark water flashed through his mind, but he pushed it aside.

"Long way," he grunted.

Henry nodded. He took off his cap and poured the last of his water over his head.

"Do you think Jason might run out on Sally?" Andrew said.

"No," Henry said. "I think he's okay. We talked while you were gone, and he feels really guilty about getting Ted to help…"

"That *was* pretty stupid." Andrew shifted on his bike seat.

Henry nodded. "Yeah, but Jason wanted to help the professor prove his theory. He's known him a long time and really respects him. Now the only way he can fix things is to get the toys back. And he's worried he's screwed up his life."

"He probably has." Andrew stashed his water bottle. "Let's go."

They rode for another mile before the buildings gave way to Shockoe Slip, its wide stretch of land spread beneath a bright blue sky that sliced through the city from northwest to southeast. It cradled Richmond's major railroad tracks and an Interstate highway, and it had steep sides laced with smaller gullies, running uphill to vacant lots.

They pedaled under a maze of overpasses, finally coasting onto a dirt road beside the railroad tracks. It was easier to get off their bikes, threading their way through the weeds and gravel until they saw a large, square metal building not too far ahead. It stood under a tall concrete bridge, and it had a row of small windows high up along one side. A fence circled behind the building, deep in the bridge's shade. A water trough stood alongside it.

"That's got to be the stable," Andrew said.

"Stop here," Henry said. "We need to tell the others we've found it and figure out what we're doing."

They backed their bikes behind some big trash bins and squatted on their heels, peering around the bins' sides. Silently they checked out the building's parking area, where a police patrol car, a small horse trailer and a traffic scooter stood next to a bright red pickup truck.

"Definitely not a police truck." Andrew felt a bug crawling up his leg and leaned over to flick it off.

But Henry was squinting at an older man dressed in khaki police clothes coming through a small door at the side of the building, carrying a bucket. He turned on a spigot next to the horse trough, filled the bucket, and went back inside. There was no sign of anyone else.

"Maybe our two guys are in there," Andrew whispered.

"I guess we have to go see," Henry said.

They grabbed their bikes and pushed them toward

the parking area's wide mesh fence, then through the gate and across the yard. They leaned their bikes against the building's wall and waited, still listening, before they moved toward the two wide-open doors at the front. Now they could see a light bulb hanging from the ceiling, shining down on a large metal table that held brushes and bridles. The table stood in front of a broad center aisle with horse stalls on either side.

Slowly, looking around one more time, Henry stepped forward and walked in, Andrew right behind him. The only sound came from several large flies, buzzing around the light bulb.

"Where is everybody?" Andrew whispered.

Andrew jumped as a deep voice came from behind his left shoulder. "Can I help you boys?"

They whirled around to see the man with the bucket, looking much bigger now that they were standing near him.

"Uh, yes, sir," Andrew stammered. "Uh, we were wondering if we could see the horses."

The police officer, for they could tell that's what he was by the patch on his short-sleeved khaki shirt, frowned. He had salt and pepper hair and a weather-beaten face.

"You boys from around here?" He asked.

Henry wondered if this was a trick question. He tried to think fast. "No, sir," he said. "We were riding our bikes from his house," he nodded at Andrew, "to my house – I live on Church Hill – and I'd always heard the stables were down here, so we decided to come and see."

The policeman looked them up and down, "Do you boys ride horses?"

"Yes sir, I do, on my grandmother's farm," Henry said, "And he" – nodding at Andrew – "wants to learn how."

"I hope you weren't thinking you could ride these horses," the officer said. "No one rides our horses except police."

"No, sir, we just wanted to see them," Andrew put in. "They look so beautiful, in parades and everything."

"You could see them if they were here," the officer said. "But I've just sent all but one off to Hanover County. We have big fields there and on nice nights my helper takes them up and turns them out to graze, where it's cool. He and his friend just left."

"Does your helper ride them?" Henry tried to sound innocent.

"No, indeed. It's fifteen miles, so he – name's Ted – trailers them up. He brought his friend along today so they went early."

Henry and Andrew exchanged excited glances. They'd found the right stable!

At that moment a loud whicker came from the back of the stalls. Henry and Andrew turned their heads.

"That's Chief," the policeman said. He got a stone in his shoe so I'm keeping him in his stall for a couple of days 'til the pain's gone. He misses his friends, but you can take a look at him if you like."

He led the way along the aisle past a number of empty stalls to one near the end of the row, where a handsome black horse was poking his head over the half door. The policeman patted his nose and the horse bobbed his head up and down, snorting happily.

"Hey, fella," the policeman said. "These boys just want to say hello." He felt in his pocket, brought out a piece of carrot and laid it flat on his palm. Delicately, Chief sniffed at it, then gently used his velvety lips to pick it up. "He's a friendly cuss," the policeman said, watching the horse crunch the carrot. "But then, all police horses have to be friendly. They do a lot of crowd work. Want to pet him?"

"Yes, sir." Andrew put his hand on Chief's glossy neck. It felt smooth and silky. "Hey, Chief, hey boy," he said.

He stepped aside to let Henry have a turn, and on a sudden impulse edged along the aisle to the next stall, at the end of the row. He peered over its half door. Hay bales stood all over the floor and wooden boxes marked 'feed' were piled high under the little window. Everything looked old and dusty. Then Andrew realized the policeman had turned to see where he was, and he edged back.

"How old is he?" Henry was asking.

"Ten," the policeman said. "Young yet." He looked at his watch "Sorry boys. I've still got work to do, but come back any time. If you come earlier in the day all the horses will be here." He waved them toward the door, but Andrew thought he seemed friendlier.

"That'd be great. Thanks a lot," Andrew said. "We will."

As they reached the stable doors Henry stopped. "Nice truck." He nodded at the red pickup.

"Belongs to Ted's friend," the policeman smiled. "Color's too bright for me."

Then he turned on his heel and went back inside, and Henry managed to walk his bike close behind the red truck. Just outside the stable yard gates he stopped and took a picture of its license number with his phone.

"Got that much, anyway," he said in a low voice. "Ted's truck is here, so he'll be back. Now we need to find a place to hide while we wait. Probably the trash bins are the best. We can see everything from there."

"I have a funny feeling about that stable," Andrew muttered, pushing his bike through a patch of chickweed. "You could hide a million things in there. Did you see that huge hayloft?"

"I did," Henry answered. He squinted back at the stable yard, now lit with slanting sunbeams. "But there's no way we could get up there now, with the guy there. I'm texting the others."

Sally answered right away. *Are you sure they'll come back to the stable?*

They have to. Henry texted back. *Their truck's here.*

Then you have to wait, she answered.

Sally and Jason were sitting on the floor of Jason's van, with the side door open. Sally slid to the sidewalk, shifting from foot to foot before she put out her legs to stretch her calf muscles. It seemed a long time since she'd done a stretch like that, or gone running either. It made her realize how hard they'd been concentrating on finding the toys. This must be what people do when they're grown up, she thought, working for days or even weeks or months on long projects, like finding a cure for a disease if they're doctors, or writing books if they're writers. Now she was learning how to do the same thing. She got back in the van and looked at Jason, who sat with his head leaning against the backside of the passenger seat, his eyes closed.

"Henry says a policeman at the stable told him Ted and his friend are up in Hanover," she said. "But they'll be coming back to the stable to get their truck, and he thinks after that they'll come home, I mean, back here."

Jason sat up with a jerk. "Sorry," he said. "Guess I was pretty tired. I didn't sleep much last night."

Sally looked at him. "When did you start helping...I mean, when did you decide to steal the toys?"

To her surprise Jason didn't look upset. He looked thoughtful. "I'm not sure exactly..." he stopped. Sally waited, but he was silent, staring off into the distance. There was almost no traffic on this side street, and she could hear a baby shrieking inside a house. Then she heard a soothing grown-up voice, and the wailing stopped.

Jason turned in his seat to face her. "I've known the professor since I was twelve. My mom worked as a secretary in the history department at his university. She's a single mom and I was an only child. She used to tell him how much I liked to read, and he would give her books for me." He sighed and looked down at his mud-splattered pants.

Sally waited. Her back itched, but she didn't dare scratch it. He might stop talking.

"When it came time for college, there was just no money. But I'd made good grades, and the professor helped me get a scholarship. A full ride." Jason swallowed hard. "And of course I took his classes. He made history so alive – like how the country got started and how all those guys risked their lives just to sign the Declaration of Independence. When he told me about his theory about the messages and how hard it was to prove, all I could think about was how could I help."

A strand of hair had fallen in Sally's face, and she pushed it back. "Do you think his theory's true? About sending messages in toys?"

"I don't know – but it makes sense. That's one of the saddest things about all this – what Ted did, I mean – now we'll probably never be able to prove the professor's theory." He clenched his fists. "If it's true, it would tell people so much more about those days. Things no one knows yet."

Sally was surprised. This Jason was not as mild as he had seemed. This Jason was full of fire, and for some reason she couldn't explain, she completely believed him.

"Well," she said, "maybe it's not over – maybe if we get the toys back, we could talk people into letting the professor try again. And let you help him."

Jason frowned. "Maybe him, but not me. I'm a nobody, a scholarship kid. And I'm the one who came up with the idea of borrowing, I mean taking, the toys, and I asked Ted to help. Nobody's going to believe I'm not as bad as he is, or that I didn't know what they were planning. Don't forget, they put the professor in the hospital."

He looked as though he was furious and about to cry at the same time, Sally thought. And she wouldn't blame him for crying tears of rage. Then he added in a choked voice, "Everything I planned for my life..." This time his voice trailed off and he got out of the van. He began walking along the sidewalk and Sally followed, feeling a new determination.

"Why are you giving up like that?" She faced him. "We haven't – Andrew and me and Henry. You shouldn't either."

He looked at her. "I know," he said. "It's just so much..."

"Look," she interrupted. "We've already found out where those guys live and work. Now we just need to find where they've hidden the toys. And if they come back here after work, we don't have to wait much longer."

But Henry and Andrew, hidden behind the trash bins, felt the afternoon was going on forever. There were no trees to shade them from the broiling sun, and the bins cut off what tiny breeze there was. The heat felt as though it was pressing them into the ground and worse, they were getting really thirsty. The sight of the spigot in the stable yard was so tantalizing Andrew had to stop looking at it. He lay stretched out in the dirt, his hair over his perspiring face, and wondered what people in the desert did when they were lost, their canteens empty, the sun frying them as they marched across huge sand dunes that stretched endlessly into the distance. They went crazy and gave up, he thought, which he definitely wasn't going to do. With a grunt he rolled over and wiped the dirt from his face. And just at that instant, he felt Henry tense.

"Something's coming," Henry said. "Look at that cloud of dust."

CHAPTER TEN

Andrew sat up, shading his eyes. Henry was half on his feet, peering around the trash bin, both of them watching the dust cloud move along the dirt road toward them. As it came closer they could see it was a big trailer, heading for the stable yard. When it got to the gate it stopped, and a man jumped out and began directing the driver.

"That's the man I saw in the museum!" Andrew almost shouted. "He was pretending to be blind!"

Henry put his finger to his lips as they watched the trailer turn, back into the yard, and edge into a slot next to the stable doors. The driver's door opened and a second man swung to the ground. "That must be Ted," Andrew said pointing to the driver. "I think he's the guy we saw on the motorcycle in front of the museum."

Henry pulled his phone from his pocket. *They're here*, he texted Sally, watching the two men walk into the stable and disappear. *We'll follow them but get ready, just in case.*

For ten long minutes they waited. Then suddenly the two men came out of the building and headed for the red pickup. Andrew and Henry were up, pushing their bikes, heading for the dirt road, but Henry veered

suddenly, swinging his bike up the steep hillside toward the bridge.

"This way's faster for us," he panted, straining up the gravelly slope. "Rush hour will slow them. We can jump in and out of the traffic."

But at the top they stopped, staring at a large sign on the bridge. It said: 'Bicycles and Pedestrians Prohibited'. The speeding traffic on four lanes of narrow roadway was impossible to cross. Andrew slammed his fist on his handlebars. "They're getting away!" he shouted.

Henry pulled out his phone again. "I'm calling Sally," he said, watching the red pickup disappear down the dirt road behind them. "Those guys'll be at the house in twenty minutes."

"Ted's on his way." Sally told Jason, putting her phone back in her shorts. "We need to hide, fast."

They hurried down the block, looking for places where they could hide and still see the pickup coming. The houses were small and close together, with tiny front yards. Thick bushes spilled out along the side walkways. Finally Jason stopped. He pointed at a shaggy-looking hedge. "There. If you stay low they can't see you."

"Where'll you be?"

"Watching. Don't worry."

He jogged away, and Sally barely had time to squat

behind the hedge before she saw a red pickup turn the corner, moving fast along the block. She bent even lower, her heart thumping, while the truck parked. She heard the doors of the truck open and slam shut, and two men talking loudly.

One of them said, "Let's eat first." His voice was loud and gruff and made Sally shudder. But it wasn't a voice she recognized. She wondered if that was the man she had seen on the motorcycle, the one called Ted. But she couldn't risk rustling the bushes until they walked away toward the porch, laughing at some joke. She heard them clomping up the steps and the front door slam, and she breathed again. Then Jason slid up on the grass beside the hedge.

"What did they say?" His voice was very quiet.

"They went in to eat," Sally answered. "And that was Ted, right?"

Jason nodded.

"What did his friend look like?" She asked.

"Tall, with long hair in a ponytail," Jason answered.

"That's the guy who pretended to be blind, the one I saw in the tire store. Wow, it's a good thing he didn't see me, I know he'd recognize me. They both would." She felt creepy, but she tried to keep her voice down.

She crawled out and moved, half crouching, up the sidewalk. "Let's get back to the van."

Jason waited until she was out of sight around the corner before he followed.

He was climbing into the driver's seat when Andrew and Henry coasted alongside and stopped.

"They've gone in the house," Sally told them. "They said they want to eat first."

"That could mean anything." Henry frowned. "You think they're home for the night?"

"Who knows," Jason said. "I found out there's no predicting those guys."

Andrew got off his bike and took off his helmet, his sweaty hair plastered to his head. "So we need to get into the house," he said, climbing in behind the others. "Maybe all four of us should knock on the door and talk to them."

Jason shook his head. "Not a good idea. They'd just laugh, and if we got in a fight, they'd win. I'm not into martial arts, and they're about a foot taller and fifty pounds heavier than you are. But you're right – we need to start with the house."

"How're we going to do that, if we don't ring the bell and get in?" Andrew sounded grumpy. His face was red and Sally knew he was upset about Jason telling them what to do.

"These houses don't have basements," Jason said. "So if we can look in Ted's windows, we might be able to see the boxes, if they're there. Put your bikes in the van and then maybe you guys could go down that alley" — he pointed — "and start in Ted's back yard. I counted, Ted's house is seven houses from this end of the block." He reached for the ignition key. "I'll drive around the block and park back a ways from their pickup. In case they decide to go somewhere I can take off right behind them. Plus, that way Sally and I can check the front rooms."

He looked at them, waiting for them to agree. A ray of late afternoon sunlight glinted on his hair, striking its red with gold. This Jason seemed like a different person, cool and determined, and older, somehow. Finally Andrew climbed out behind Henry and hoisted his bike into the van.

"Look," Henry said when the van had disappeared around the corner. "We're all in this. No one person is going to get the toys back."

"I know, but I don't like him bossing us around," Andrew said.

"He's not." Henry started walking. "He's got good ideas."

"Maybe," Andrew said, "but this is our case, and I'm not letting him take it over."

They jogged into the alley, slowing down over its cobblestones and ducking under overhanging tree branches. At a tall brown gate, Henry stopped.

"I think this is seven," he said, trying the latch. It was locked. He half jumped at the gate, his feet scrabbling for a foothold. He got his toes on the latch and pushed himself up, looking over the top. The yard was mostly grass, stretching between the back fence and the house, which had two windows facing the alley. A rickety air conditioner hung under one of them. The windows were wide open.

"Cross your fingers those guys aren't looking outside," Henry whispered. "Here goes."

He slithered over and Andrew dove after him, landing behind a row of bushes growing against the fence. Breathing hard, they kept still. When nothing happened, Henry said, "We don't have to cross the grass if we stay behind these bushes and follow them all the way around."

Minutes later they were flat against the back wall of the house, and Henry pointed at the window above them.

"Stand on my hands," he whispered, locking his fingers together.

Andrew stepped up, grabbing the air conditioner. Very slowly he moved his head above it. When his eyes came even with the top his heart gave a lurch. The man he had seen on the motorcycle, the one who must be Ted, was sitting on a shabby sofa not ten feet away, his feet propped on a table in front of him, staring at a big TV screen across the room. Two large pizzas and some beer bottles sat on the table, and the other man with the ponytail was just turning away from the refrigerator with more beer bottles in his hands.

Andrew ducked just in time. "They're right here," he whispered, "watching TV and eating pizza." For a minute he tried not to think how long it had been since they'd had chicken and apples at home.

"Switch with me." Henry eased up to look. He stayed

a little longer, slowly turning his head to see the whole room. Then he stepped back down.

"No boxes," he said. "Let's try the side windows."

Andrew's phone vibrated, making them both jump. Sally.

"What's happening?" she asked.

"They're eating and watching TV," Andrew whispered. "Nothing's in the kitchen. You see anything?"

"Just the living room," she said. "Only old beat-up furniture."

The phone buzzed again. Andrew looked at it and frowned. "Mac," he whispered to Sally.

"Answer her." Sally said. "She'll get suspicious."

"She yells," Andrew whispered. He looked nervously up at the windows and pushed the volume button down as far as he could. "Hi, Mac," he said in a low voice.

"Your mom said you might be late," Mac shouted, so loud Henry looked over and shook his head.

"Do you know when you'll be home? I have to study, Business/Econ exam tomorrow. I can leave your plates in the oven, but if you're going to be really late I'd appreciate your re-heating them when you get here. Don't like to leave the stove on."

"Fine," Andrew whispered, wondering when Mac would realize they were old enough to get their own supper. "Thanks."

He looked at Henry, who was smiling, his hand on his stomach, but then they both heard one of the men speaking and Andrew rose up a little to listen. The voice stopped, and Andrew jumped down and crouched beside Henry, easing his way along the wall. "He said 'we can wait awhile longer. We don't need to go right now. Let's watch some baseball'."

"Okay," Henry said. "Let's find the others. We can get to the sidewalk along this side of the house."

Sally met them halfway. "Now what?" She said.

Andrew dropped back and waited. "I've thought of something else," he said in a low voice.

"What?"

"I'm going back to the police stables. I'm sure that's where the toys are. I've been thinking about it all afternoon."

She was quiet for a minute. Then she said, "That's really risky, especially at night. I think we should see what Ted does first."

"That's just it," Andrew said. "Ted's not doing anything right now, so this is a perfect time. And if I ride really fast I can get there and back before it gets dark. If he leaves, you all can chase him, or call the police."

Suddenly a Mockingbird began to sing, sitting in the branches of a big crepe myrtle bush right next to them. Startled, they stopped talking, listening until the bird's song melted into the soft sounds of the late afternoon. Then it flew away, and Sally looked at Andrew. "You can't go by yourself."

"Of course I can," he answered. "No one's there at

night, and I know how to get in. There's a back window that's open, with only a wire screen on it."

Almost to herself, Sally said, "We'd have to be quick."

"What do you mean, 'we'?" Andrew said. But he already knew. She'd made up her mind to come with him, and he knew nothing he could say would stop her. When he thought about it, that wasn't all bad.

"Let's find the others," he said, heading for the van.

"Good idea," Henry said when Andrew told them, and Jason nodded. "You'll need stuff," he said, and began rummaging in his glove compartment. He pulled out a flashlight and a pair of wire clippers from his tool kit, and then he walked around and opened the back doors, pulling out an unopened bag of pretzels and a granola bar.

"You can have those too." He grinned at them, and Andrew actually grinned back.

They pulled their bikes out and put on their helmets, and Andrew adjusted his helmet strap. "I guess that's everything then," he said. "We can go."

"We'll tell you what these guys do," Henry said, "but text us a lot?"

Sally nodded. "We will. Don't worry." The sun was slowly going down, throwing up pale lavender and pink clouds. She wondered what Shockoe Slip's vacant lots and streets would be like when it got dark, and if there were any streetlights. But as they headed out they didn't talk, saving their energy for pedaling fast. It was still very hot and Sally looked up to see clouds drawing water from the sun. Dad used to say that meant rain, but she couldn't remember how soon the rain was supposed to come. When they turned onto Broad Street she pulled alongside Andrew.

"I know you don't like Jason much, she said, "but I talked to him about stuff this afternoon, and I can tell he's really trying."

"But I don't want him running things," Andrew said. "He could screw us up."

"Not if we don't let him," she answered. "Right now we need him, at least to watch Ted 'til we get back."

At Meadow Street they turned east, flying across the streets until Andrew pulled up, panting. "Jackson Ward's over there." He pointed even further east. Sally knew that was an Historic District, with a lot of Citizen Patrols. "We've got to be really careful through there. We don't want to be seen by the police or anybody else."

Past Jackson Ward they were in deserted territory, where any children alone, especially ones with nice bicycles, would stand out. As if it had read Sally's thoughts, a police car suddenly came out of a side street and drove slowly toward them. Andrew tried not to look up, but he could sense it was braking. He kept pedaling, but before he could get by, the driver's window went down and a uniformed arm came out, waving at them to stop.

Sally pulled alongside Andrew and looked at the

two policemen in the front seat. The one who was driving smiled. "Hi there," he said.

"Hi," they both answered.

"Can you tell me where you kids are going?" He said.

For a minute they felt caught. What reason could they possibly have, on these empty streets?

The policeman tried again. "Where do you kids live?"

"On Monument Avenue," Sally said.

Andrew added, "We're going to see a friend." He pointed across the Slip. "He lives over there."

What's his address?" The policeman's tone was still reasonable, but Sally could tell it wouldn't be much longer. She crossed her fingers. "Officer, he's sick. We don't know his house number, it's on Chamberlayne Avenue."

"Your parents know you're going?" He said.

Andrew's voice was firm. "Yes," he said, crossing his fingers behind his back.

The policeman gave them a long look, but then he nodded. "It'd be best if you turn around and go up to the Boulevard. Take that to get there. I know it's longer but it's safer. And when you go home tonight you can take the Boulevard too. This place is kind of rough, especially at night. You don't want to be here by yourselves."

"We will," Sally said, starting to turn around. "Thank you."

He waved and the car started to move. "Be careful," they heard him call back.

They pedaled slowly back until they were sure the car had gone, and then Andrew stopped. "We don't have time to go that way," he said. "It's much longer."

He turned around, Sally beside him, and ten minutes later they reached Shockoe Slip's wide, deep ravine. They halted at the top of the steep slope, looking at the Interstate and the railroad tracks spread out below them.

"There's our dirt road." Andrew pointed, and she could see it in the distance beside the nearest railroad track. "The stable's at the end."

He was already starting down the side of the ravine, sliding on the clay and gravel. Sally got off her bike, her arm muscles straining to keep it from getting away and crashing to the bottom. Somehow she got down, and now she could see the stable in the distance. She didn't know what she'd expected, but not this gloomy-looking building in front of them, standing under the shadow of a tall overpass.

"It looks so, I don't know, empty," she said. "Are there any horses inside?"

"A couple, but they take most of them up to a pasture in the country at night." Andrew started to push his bike along the dirt road. "That's why I said no one would be here."

Even so, when they got to the parking area gate, he stood for a minute or two, looking and listening. The last rays of the sun had already left the stable yard, and the whole area was shrouded in shadow, though there was still enough light to see that nothing moved. In spite of the distant sounds of traffic on the overpass, a deep silence seemed to have fallen on the land around them. They went through the gate without speaking, circling their bikes around two empty horse trailers. Sally felt a surge of relief when she saw a lone light hanging over the building's front entrance. At least there'd be some light if they needed it later, just in case, she thought. Andrew had rounded the corner of the building, and Sally could see a row of small windows, high up on the wall. She looked across the railroad track, wondering if anyone was watching. Beyond the track the ravine rose steeply, covered with thick Kudzu vines and laced with clay gullies, worn deep by rain. No one was in sight. Even the railroad track didn't look as though many trains used it. When Andrew reached the end of the building, he pulled his bike underneath the last window. It was propped open, its wire screen sagging a little.

"I can stand on my bike seat," he whispered. "Hold the handlebars."

He pulled out his wire cutters and flashlight and hooked them to his belt. But when he looked up again his face fell. He could tell that even standing on the seat he wouldn't be tall enough.

"Maybe I can do it," Sally said. "Hold the bike."

She put one foot on the chain bar and grabbed

Andrew's shoulder. She got her other foot onto one of the handlebars and dug her fingers between the building's metal slats. Slowly, she straightened up. She raised her arm and her fingers touched the wire screen.

"Great!" Andrew whispered.

"Clippers," she whispered back.

He held them up and she leaned down to get them, grabbing his head to keep her balance. It took three tries to hook the clippers onto one of the wire strands, but at last, squeezing hard, she felt a crack as the wire snapped.

She hooked the next wire, snapped, and when she reached the last one Andrew could hear scraping sounds as she pushed the screen in. Then, carefully, she lowered her cramped arms. The handlebar wobbled.

"Don't do that! I can't hold it!" Andrew hissed.

"You have to," she hissed back. "But I'm not sure I can get up to the window sill to get in."

"You can if we find something taller to stand on," he said, rubbing his shoulder. He looked around, worried. It was much closer to dark than he'd thought.

Sally was getting down. "What about that big barrel over there?" She pointed at the corral fence. "If we can find something to put on top of it, it'd be high enough."

It took both of them to tilt the barrel sideways and roll it to the building, and once they got it there it was even harder to turn upside down. But its bottom was solid and strong enough to stand on, and they found a cinderblock to add more height.

"That's good enough," Sally said. "I'll go first, I'm older."

"But I've been inside," Andrew said. "I know what it's like."

She looked at him. Then she bent over and locked her hands together. "Okay," she said. "Go."

"Wait." He said. "We need to hide our bikes, just in case."

The stable yard was bare, but Sally grabbed her bike and started toward the back of the building.

"No, the horse trailers," Andrew said.

She turned around. "Right."

The only sounds were the far off traffic on the overpass and a Mourning Dove, calling from the top of the ravine across the railroad track. Andrew moved forward, reached the nearest trailer, and shoved his bike inside, Sally's behind it. They pulled the door partly closed and stood back to look.

"Perfect," Sally said. "Let's go." She was feeling edgy, partly because she'd never thought getting inside the stable would take this long.

Under the window, Andrew stepped into her hands and onto the barrel. This time he reached the sill easily, and for a minute he lay there on his stomach, letting his eyes adjust to the dim light inside. He could make out the straw bales piled around the sides of the stall underneath him, and he heard a faint whicker. Chief, he thought, sliding further inside. Of course. The black horse's stall was right next to this one.

He reached for his flashlight, but it was in the pocket he was lying on. He tried rolling sideways, but the little window was too small.

"Do you see anything?" Sally called in a low voice.

"Only the horse," he answered. "I'm going in."

And with one last push to get his shoulders through, he slid through the opening and dropped into the blackness below.

CHAPTER ELEVEN

For a minute Sally stood motionless, the quiet broken only by a distant rumbling of trucks across the overpass. Then Andrew's voice, sounding hollow, floated up through the little window.

"You can come," she heard. "It's fine in here."

She took a quick look around, climbed onto the cinderblock and grabbed the sill. She pulled herself up to it and looked inside.

Andrew stood right below her, halfway up to his knees in straw. "Jump." He pointed at the bale of hay he'd shoved under the window.

A minute later she was on the floor beside him. Something close by whickered and she saw a velvety muzzle poking through the bars of the next stall. Before Dad died she'd taken riding lessons, and the sight made her remember how much she'd loved horses.

"That's Chief," Andrew said. "I think he's lonely."

"He's beautiful," she said, patting Chief's muzzle. "We should have brought him a carrot."

But Andrew was already scrambling up the stall door to reach down on the outside and shove back the latch. The door clicked open, and she followed him out into the aisle.

"You take the stalls on that side," Andrew said. "I'll take these."

They hurried in and out of every stall, shining their flashlights' beams in the corners and along the walls, the light flicking over feed baskets and water buckets and the straw padding the floors. But all the stalls were empty, and at the end of the row they came to a stop by the big front doors. Another smaller door stood on their left. "That's a tack room," Andrew said. "It was open when we were here this afternoon. It's only a bunch of saddles in there."

Sally pointed to a wooden ladder in a corner against the building's wall. "What's that?"

He peered up toward the ceiling. "I think it's the ladder to the hayloft. We need to get up there."

He ran over and put one foot on the first rung, which felt solid. Sally followed him, and at the top their flashlights flickered around a huge room piled high with hay. A big pitchfork lay on the floor, and Andrew began thrusting it into the nearest pile, throwing the hay behind him.

Sally propped her light on an old wooden stool and headed for another pile, using her hands to pull the hay loose. They worked silently for a few minutes, but then Sally straightened up and brushed her hair from her face.

"There's no way we can dig all this straw out tonight," she said.

Andrew had built up a steady rhythm, digging,

lifting, throwing back, digging, lifting, throwing back. "We have to," he panted. "That's why we came. You can go home if you want, but I'm staying."

She looked at him, wondering how she'd been born with such a stubborn brother. "I'm not going home," she said.

Before she could answer, her phone vibrated. Henry. *Done eating. Looks like they're getting ready to go out. Jason's in his van & I'm outside hiding.*

She looked at Andrew. "He thinks they're getting ready to move."

"So keep working," Andrew said, but five minutes later her phone rang.

Henry's voice sounded strained. "They're leaving." There was a pause, then he said, "Hold on…" he stopped again.

"What? WHAT?" Sally was shouting.

"Jason's tire's gone flat," Henry said. "And we heard those guys say they're on their way to the stables."

Sally whirled. "They're coming!"

"Get down the ladder, quick!" Andrew threw his pitchfork into a corner and headed for the opening.

Sally rushed after him, her mind racing. "Our bikes. And they'll see the barrel," she panted. "We've got to get out of here."

"No, we don't." Andrew was down and turning in a circle. "We hid the bikes and that barrel looks normal. Just hide somewhere they won't think of looking."

Sally peered at the stalls. She saw Chief watching them, his head poking over his half door. "Him!" She pointed. "We can hide in his stall! They'll never think of that!"

"Maybe…" Andrew frowned. "What if he kicks us or something?"

"He's not going to kick us." She was hurrying down the aisle, snatching a handful of feed from a box propped against the wall. "Come on, this'll work."

"He might knock us over," Andrew said, still uneasy.

"He won't," Sally said, trying to remember more about horses from her lessons. "I'll go first."

She stood in the door, lifting the feed up to Chief's muzzle. His lips snuffled over her palm as he ate it, and slowly she moved her hand up to his head and caught hold of his halter, patting his neck with her other hand. I think I remember how to do this, she thought, using his halter to push and pull him backwards into the middle of the stall, which smelled of horse and straw. "He likes us," she said, letting out her breath. "You were right, he was lonely."

"Maybe, but don't let go of him," Andrew said, squeezing in behind her. In this small space the horse looked even bigger.

"I have to," Sally said. "They'll see me. Hurry, text Henry where we are."

Andrew pulled the door shut and climbed up to latch it. He edged carefully around to the back wall and crouched down, pulling out his phone. Chief was still snorting and nudging at Sally. She let go of his halter, ready to grab it back, but he only wanted to nose around in the straw on the bottom of the stall and take a few steps to his water bucket. Sally moved back beside Andrew just as a bright flash of headlights flared through the cracks in the stable's front doors. A vehicle screeched to a halt outside, and Sally and Andrew dropped to the floor.

"It's them," Andrew whispered.

Truck doors slammed, and they heard the stable doors slide open, rattling loudly. Suddenly the aisle was lit with glaring lights, and voices echoed inside the building. Sally was holding her breath so hard she was starting to see spots. She let it out, knowing she had to stay calm. The door to the tack room opened and closed with a clang. Chief's ears pricked up, and Andrew eased over to a place where he could see through a crack in the stall's boards. He turned to Sally and pointed upwards. The men were going up the hayloft ladder. She flattened herself as low as she could, and Andrew scuttled back beside her.

"I'm going out the window. I can get to their tires," he whispered.

"No!" She hissed. "That's way too dangerous. One of them might come down and see you!"

"It's too dangerous not to," he barely breathed back. "You know the toys must be in the hayloft. Once those guys get them in the truck they're gone. If I go now, I can do it."

He was already inching to the corner, where he scrabbled for a foothold and slithered up and over the partition into the stall next door. Chief snorted quietly, and Sally patted his nose. She could hear a soft rustling as Andrew piled more hay bales under the little window, and a slight banging when his feet flailed for a place under the window to push himself up, and a small creak as he bent the wire further back. Then, nothing. He'd done it. He was out.

In the silence Sally heard thumps coming from above her head and then dragging noises, as though a large object was being moved across the floor. She sucked in her breath, trying to decide what to do. Text Henry, she thought, but suddenly she saw a man's legs on the ladder. He was backing unsteadily down its rungs, and a second man's legs came into view above him. They were carrying a big carton, and instantly, she knew what was in it.

The toys.

For a minute she couldn't move. Then, hot rage shot through her whole body. Here, right in front of her, these men were about to put boxes loaded with her mother's wonderful exhibit in a truck and take them away! Not if I can help it, she thought, so furious her legs started to shake. She forced herself to breathe calmly while the two men reached the bottom and put the box down. Then they started back up the ladder and Sally made herself think, hard. She had no way to reach Andrew, and even if he had gotten to the truck's tires, how long would that stop the men?

Andrew had gotten there, creeping along the outside wall and stopping for only a second before he ran behind the back of the red pickup. Crouching down, he realized he needed something to open the tire's air valve, but all he had were the wire cutters and the flashlight, and they were too big. Then he thought of his phone and pulled off its back. It was very thin, and if he could get its corner into the valve...he leaned over the back tire and pushed the little metal piece in. It turned! Air was hissing out when a harsh voice said, "Hey! Get away from there!"

Andrew jumped back, rising to his feet, but the man was too quick and grabbed both his arms. He pushed his unshaven face close to Andrew's. His breath smelled of cigarette smoke and beer. "What do you think you're doing?" He shouted.

Andrew widened his eyes, trying to look innocent. He could hear his heart hammering in his chest. "Just—just having some fun," he stammered in his best little kid voice.

"Yeah, right. Lucky I came outside for a smoke," the man said, tightening his grip and propelling Andrew into the stable. "Here. Have some fun in there."

He gave a hard shove, and Andrew lurched into the tack room, almost hitting his head on the opposite wall. The door slammed and the lock clicked. He reached for his phone, and his heart sank when he saw the battery was gone. He'd dropped the back cover when the guy jerked him off the ground, and the battery must have fallen out too. He threw himself at the door and started pounding on it, yelling at the top of his lungs.

Sally froze when she heard him. "Oh, no," she whispered. "Now what do I do?"

Get outside fast, she thought. *There's nothing I can do for Andrew in here.*

But how? They might see her trying to get out the little window. The noise had made Chief uneasy, and he nudged her again. "It's okay, boy," she whispered, patting his neck and smoothing his mane. He gave a friendly little whicker, and as she looked at him, a wild thought came out of nowhere. What if she let him loose, and he ran away? Henry had said Ted took care of the horses, so Ted would have to go after him, wouldn't he? And maybe the pretend blind guy too? That could get them away from the stable, and maybe give her time to get Andrew out.

But then she shook her head. Even if she let Chief loose, he might not run away. He might just hang around the stable. And then another thought came right behind the first. "If I...," she whispered slowly,... "if I could get up on him..." And suddenly she knew exactly what she was going to do. Ride him. Ride him out of the stable as fast as he could go, and as far away from Ted as they could get.

Before she could change her mind she reached for his

halter, led him to the sidewall and braced one foot against the boards. She climbed up and taking a deep breath she jumped, landing squarely on his back. Remembering her lessons she tightened her legs, and he took two nervous steps. She reached over the stall door, undid the latch, and the door swung outwards. She hesitated only a second before she grabbed his mane and slammed her heels against his sides. Chief leapt forward with a startled snort, flying through the door and thundering down the aisle, just as the men started forward with the next carton.

The horse came straight at them, swerving just in time, but not before the pretend blind guy dropped his side of the box and fell backwards. The heavy container landed on top of him and he yelled in pain as Sally and Chief roared past and out the front door. They were through the stable yard and on the dirt road before she knew it, going at an astonishing speed. She was holding the sides of Chief's neck with all her might, her heart beating so hard she could barely breathe. She tried straightening up and tightening her legs, but the more she gripped him with her knees, the faster he went.

She heard shouts behind them, and scared as she was, it sounded like her plan was working — Ted was chasing after them, which meant he'd leave Andrew alone for the moment. But if Chief stopped, she thought... until she realized he wasn't about to slow down; he was going like the wind through the darkening twilight, and if she could just hang on they might actually get away.

But hanging on was getting harder because the faster he went, the more she slid from side to side on his bare back. Her legs were all that were keeping her from sliding all the way off, and now they were getting tired from gripping him so hard. Her arms were cramping too, and she risked letting go one hand to grab his mane. But the long black hairs slipped through her fingers, and she felt herself bouncing backwards, no longer able to hold onto any part of him. I can't fall off, she thought, I can't. But another set of bounces told her it was about to happen, and in two more minutes she was almost over Chief's tail. Then she felt nothing under her but air before she slammed onto the ground with a hard thud, all the breath knocked out of her.

For a minute she didn't move, slowly getting her breath back and almost not believing what had just happened. Then, carefully, she wiggled each arm and each leg. She raised her head and moved it in circles. It only felt a little jarred, and nothing else really hurt. To her surprise Chief was standing across the road, snorting and looking at her, almost as though he was waiting for her. Suddenly she felt a rush of affection for this large, beautiful creature, and then she remembered she had to hide him, fast. Just because the shouting had died away and the road behind them was empty didn't mean Ted wasn't close behind.

She got slowly to her feet, her legs feeling shaky from the strain of gripping Chief's sides. She walked over to rub Chief's nose and pat his neck. "We've got to find a hiding place," she said, looking around,

Ahead on the left a little gully slanted up the bank, with a rough, steep path zigzagging to the top. Maybe she could get him up there and even further back from the road, out of sight and out of earshot. She wondered if he would follow her — or if she could lead him. She broke off a piece of vine from the sand bank by the road and slid it through his halter, tugging him forward. He took a few steps and another tug got him plunging straight up the gully and over the top of the bank, where a clump of trees stood outlined against the twilit sky. They were dark and spooky-looking, but Sally pushed her way under their branches, pulling Chief into a little clearing. She could leave him here, she thought, crossing her fingers he wouldn't break loose until she could get back. And he seemed happy, only wanting to put his head down and start nibbling at a patch of grass.

"We'll come back for you, don't worry," she whispered, thankful the vine was long enough to give him room to move around a little. She tied its end to a sturdy-looking branch, gave him a final pat, and hurried out of the trees to listen for Ted. A freight train whistled far up Shockoe Slip, crickets chirped loudly and the hot night breeze carried a scent of damp, cool earth, but she heard no shouts or sounds of running feet. Maybe Ted had given up and gone back. Or maybe he had just gone silent, thinking that would be a better way to catch them.

Get to Andrew, she thought. That's the first thing. Find Henry and Jason. As though her phone had read her thoughts, it buzzed. She pulled it out of her shorts. Henry.

"Where *are* you?" He was whispering. "I'm here. Jason's on his way."

"You're here?" Sally's voice squeaked. "Where?"

"Up on the bank by the trash bins, on my bike. There's a guy standing in the stable door, carrying a big electric lantern. I think it's Ted. Looks like he's got a spotlight too, hooked on his belt."

Sally took a deep breath and as fast as she could, she told him everything. "We've got to wreck their truck or something. And get Andrew out," she finished. "They might hurt him."

"Right," Henry said. He was quiet for a minute. Then he said, "did you actually see the toys?"

"Well, no, I didn't actually see them, but what else could be in that big carton?"

"I don't know," he said, "You're probably right." He was quiet again, thinking. "Should we call the police now, or our parents…? You know they're going to start wondering soon."

An owl hooted across the railroad tracks, a welcoming sound in the soft night air. Sally breathed in the sweet scent of honeysuckle on the bank beside her, and all of a sudden she was absolutely sure she didn't want to call anybody. Standing here, even though she'd just crashed off of a horse, she couldn't believe everything she'd done. And I'm not stopping now, she thought, not until we get the toys and pay Ted and that pretend blind guy back for what they've done.

"Sally?" Henry's voice came through the speaker. "Sally? Are you there?"

She blinked, her mind coming back to the muddy bank. "I'm here," she said, almost too loudly. "And no. Don't call yet. We've got another hour or so before they start to worry. You're right we don't know for sure what's in those boxes, so we need to find out before we get the police and everybody else over here. I don't want those guys to run away if they hear the police sirens. Besides, we can get to Andrew faster than the police can. Just wait there – I'm coming."

"Okay, but hurry. And make sure they don't see you." He hung up.

In the dark it was much harder to go down the gully than climb up, but the moon and stars were out and Sally could see well enough to run. Even so it seemed a long time before the stable's lights appeared in the distance. One light was flashing just outside its gates. That was probably Ted, she thought. He must have gone back for a lantern after it got really dark, and now he was heading out on their trail again. Except he was standing still, looking up at the trash bins. As she came closer, she saw what he was staring at – Henry, sitting on his bike, looking down. She ran faster, ducking behind a big bush just as Henry hurtled down the slope on his bike, aiming right for Ted.

CHAPTER TWELVE

Just in time Ted jumped out of the way, kicking the bike sideways with a crash. "What do you think you're doing?" He yelled.

Henry was on his feet before Ted could move again, calmly brushing dirt off his T-shirt. "What do *you* think you're doing?" he said. "Knocking my bike over like that."

"You were coming straight at me!" Ted sounded very angry.

"I couldn't help it if my brakes wouldn't hold," Henry said coolly. "They need fixing."

Ted stared at him silently. After about a minute he asked, "Those kids your friends?"

Sally sucked in her breath, watching Henry look around.

"What kids?" he said. "I don't see any kids. I'm taking a short cut home." He picked up his bike, but Ted stepped in front of him.

"Listen. Now that you're here, you help me for a little while, there's ten bucks in it for you."

"Ten dollars!" Henry laughed. "What'd that buy? Anyway, I'm not looking for work," he added, getting back on his seat.

"Twenty, then," Ted said, looking at Henry's bike.

"I can see you've got an eye for expensive equipment. Maybe that'll be enough to fix your brakes."

"What's the job?" Henry asked, sounding bored. Sally grinned. She didn't think she knew anyone this cool.

"Help my friend Mike load some boxes into that red pickup," Ted said. "While I go find a horse and the girl that's riding him."

Suddenly from inside the stable, they heard a loud clanging noise, and someone yelling.

Henry started to edge away. "Something's going on here," he said.

"Nothing's going on," Ted said. "I work here. I came back tonight to check the horses and move some freight. Lucky I did, I caught a couple of kids here. One of 'em's shut up in the tack room – that's him banging on the door. The other one's trying to steal a horse." His voice took on a menacing edge.

Henry looked around again. "Well okay, I'll load your boxes, if it won't take too long. Where are they?"

Ted nodded at the stable. "In there. Mike's a little bit hurt, but he'll get over it. Go tell him I hired you." He was already moving toward the gate, and Sally jumped back just before the beam from his lantern reached her bush. "I'll be back when I get the horse," Ted called back. "This is a police stable. I could lose my job if I don't find him."

As soon as the dark swallowed his bobbing light,

Sally dashed for the stable doors. The overhead bulb shone along the aisle where Henry was walking between the stalls toward a man sitting on the floor. Mike, the pretend blind guy. She shuddered and flattened herself against the wall, knowing he'd recognize her if he saw her. But at the moment he was holding his stomach with one hand, and rubbing his hip with the other. "Who're you?" he growled at Henry.

"Hank." Henry gestured behind him. "Your friend out there hired me to help you load some boxes. He's gone after a horse."

Mike rolled on his side and groaned. "I need a minute," he said.

"Take your time, man," Henry said. "Where're the boxes?"

"There's one down here, the one that fell on me. The others're up there." Mike pointed to the ladder.

"Okay," Henry said. "Maybe I can do some of it myself."

"Nah, I'm okay." Mike struggled to his feet. He stood for a minute before he limped over and took a step up the ladder, Henry behind him. Moving slowly, they got to the top and Mike heaved himself through the opening. Henry looked back at Sally and gave a tiny wave before he disappeared too, and Sally turned and ran to the tack room door. She turned the key and Andrew rushed out, holding a small screwdriver.

"I'll try and disable the truck," he whispered.

"Hurry," she whispered back. "We need to help Henry." She pointed at the ladder, but Andrew was already out the front doors.

She crept halfway up to listen, but the voices above sounded muffled. Carefully Sally raised her head through the opening, an inch at a time. Mike was facing away from her toward a back corner, kicking the hay and pointing at a pitchfork.

"Hand me that," she heard him say to Henry. "You can dig with your hands. We got to get three more boxes out."

He began forking the hay aside while Henry pulled it away into the corner. Suddenly Mike's pitchfork made a loud pinging noise.

"Okay, here's the next one," he said. "Help me pick it up."

"What's in it?" Henry asked.

Mike's voice changed. "None of your business, is it?" He growled.

"It is," Henry said. "If I got to carry stuff, I need to be careful with it, don't I?"

"Yeah, I guess so," Mike said. "It's just some old toys. Taking 'em to some kids' camp or something."

Sure you are, Henry thought, but he only said, "Let's do it, then."

Sally ducked as Henry and Mike picked up the box and began moving toward her and the ladder. At the opening Mike stopped for a minute, breathing heavily, and rested the box on the floor. Henry pulled out his phone.

"Put that away," Mike grunted. "Might lose it in the hay."

"Just checking the time," Henry said smoothly. "I'm supposed to be home."

"So now you've checked. Put it away," Mike said in a menacing voice.

Henry stared at him. "Who're you, boss of the world? I don't have to do this, man. You can load your own boxes."

"Yeah, well, maybe you *shouldn't* do this!" Mike sneered. His face reddened. "You're asking too many questions. With a quick move he knocked Henry's arm and the phone slid to the floor.

"Hey! Henry shouted. "That's my new phone! You can't do that!"

"I just did." Mike brought his fist up, hard, under Henry's nose. "You probably stole it, anyway. Now pick up that box before I knock you down that ladder too."

Henry didn't move. Mike lunged at him but Henry was faster, stepping to the side and sticking out his foot. Mike fell forward, his pitchfork landing at Henry's feet. In a flash Henry had it in his hands, pointing it at Mike's chest.

"You do that again, I'll use this," he said.

"Crazy punk," Mike yelled, struggling to roll away and flailing with his arms to get up on one knee. He glared at Henry, his face still red with rage. "I'll get you for this."

Henry reached down to grab his phone. "Not now you won't," he said, shifting the pitchfork closer. "Right now we're going downstairs."

Mike didn't move, and Henry raised the pitchfork, fast. "I said, go downstairs."

"Maybe you want us to push you?" Sally's voice came from the top of the ladder. "My pitchfork's even bigger than his."

She hoped he didn't hear the way her voice quavered, but he only swiveled around to stare at her. After a minute he struggled up and limped toward the opening. With Henry above and Sally below, he started down the ladder.

At the bottom, clutching his injured leg, he stared at Andrew, standing in the aisle. "You'll pay for this," he growled. "When Ted gets back here you'll pay all right."

Henry took a step forward, raising his pitchfork. "Get in the tack room," he said, jerking his head toward Andrew, who opened the door. Mike laughed. "Are you crazy? Bunch of kids. How you gonna make me?"

Henry's quick jab hit Mike's ribs hard, too fast for the older man to dodge. He yelled in pain as Sally and Andrew grabbed his arms and shoved him backward through the door. Andrew slammed it shut and locked it, and Henry took a deep breath.

"Okay." He tapped his phone. "Now we find Jason."

Where r u? He texted.

Almost there, Jason answered. *Traffic.*

Hurry. Henry texted. *We've got a problem.*

"I'm calling Mom," Sally said. She looked at her brother. "You call the police."

But a hard voice from the stable doors said, "No, he's not calling anybody. Drop your phones, all of you, now."

They whirled. Ted stood in the entrance doors. One of his hands held Chief by the vine rope, and the other held a pistol, pointed straight at them.

They froze. None of them had ever seen a pistol, except in the movies or on TV, and this one looked different. It was dark gray.

"Drop the phones, I said. You, too!" Ted snarled at Henry.

"What do you mean, me too?" Somehow Henry kept his voice calm. "I'm working for you, remember? I don't know these guys, but if we're not loading the boxes, I want my money."

"So where's Mike?" Ted looked around.

"They shut him in there." Henry nodded at the tack room door.

"And you let them?" Ted said.

"They had pitchforks," Henry said. "I'm not here to get hurt. I don't know what's going on, but I want my money."

"Well you're not getting any," Ted said. "I don't

know what your game is, but I don't see any boxes down here, so you're out of luck."

Leading Chief, he walked forward until he was standing right in front of them. His breathing sounded very loud in the silence.

"Which one of you's been fooling with my truck?" His voice was dangerously quiet, his pistol very steady. Sally had never seen anyone look so angry. For an awful minute she thought he might really shoot them.

"Well actually, I was," Henry said, not looking at Andrew. "I thought these guys might steal it."

But Andrew interrupted. "No, it was me. I was trying to stop you taking our Mom's toys." Sally couldn't believe how angry he sounded.

"You don't know what you're talking about," Ted sneered. "Your mother's toys?"

But Andrew didn't back down. "Everyone knows what you did," he said. "You and your friend stole them from that professor and beat him up."

"Shut up," Ted said. "And go unlock that door." He waved the pistol.

"What door?" Andrew said, his voice almost steady.

Ted raised the pistol. "Don't play dumb. You want me to shoot you?"

This couldn't be happening, Sally thought, not to my brother! "Leave him alone!" She screamed at Ted.

She took two quick steps in front of Andrew, trying to push him behind her, but before Ted could move a horrendous crash reverberated through the metal building, rattling the walls and doors with a loud roaring noise that echoed down the aisle. Chief reared, squealing with fear, his forelegs flailing wildly in the air. He yanked Ted sideways as he plunged forward and whirled, sending one of his rear hooves into a metal bucket. Almost crazed he began to jump from side to side, banging the bucket against the floor. He reared again, but Ted was holding his rope so tightly that he lunged sideways and came down hard against Ted's shoulder, knocking them both into the wall.

For a few seconds Ted pushed frantically with his arms, trying to ward off the thrashing horse. But then, very slowly, he began to slide down the wall under Chief's raking hooves. The rope fell out of his hand and a hoof struck his arm. The pistol flew up in the air and landed on the floor.

Andrew got to it first, diving and rolling over and up on his feet, pointing the pistol straight at Ted. "Don't move," he said in his best police show voice. He looked amazingly calm, and Sally stifled a crazy urge to giggle.

"Put that down," Ted yelled, but he stayed on the ground. "You know you won't shoot anybody."

"Oh, but he would," Sally said loudly. "He's a trained marksman," she went on, knowing she was babbling. "He shot a deer last fall, right between the eyes."

"That's true." They heard another voice, Jason's voice, coming down the aisle. He grinned at Ted. "That

kid'll shoot, all right. Except now it's my turn." He moved forward beside Andrew, who handed him the pistol.

There was a sudden silence, broken by Chief's nervous snuffling where he stood near his stall, his sides still heaving. Then they heard sirens, distant at first, quickly growing louder.

"I figured it was time to call the police," Jason said, his eyes locked on Ted. "It's not like you can get away. I just crashed into your truck." His voice hardened. "And if you move even one inch, I really will shoot."

No one moved except Henry, who grabbed a lead line from a hook and dropped it over Ted's shoulders. They could hear police cars tearing into the stable yard, tires squealing, red and blue lights flashing. The cars screeched to a stop, and what looked to Andrew like enough policemen for a baseball team scrambled out and ran into the stable doors.

Only then did Jason step to one side so the police could grab Ted's arms and Andrew could hand the nearest officer the key to the tack room.

"There's another guy in there." He pointed at the door. "We locked him in."

The policeman looked startled. Then he grinned. "You guys have been busy," he said.

"Yeah, we have," Andrew answered, feeling proud.

"We had help from a friend," Sally said. "We couldn't have done it without him. He crashed his van into that guy's truck to stop him." She nodded toward Ted, who the police were putting into one of the cars. "And *he* had that gun." She pointed at it on a hay bale against the wall. She was looking around. "Where'd Jason go?" She said to Andrew in a low voice.

"Not sure," Andrew said. "He was here a minute ago."

"Out front." Henry started for the doors behind two officers, who were marching Mike out to a squad car. Sally and Andrew ran behind him, blinking in the bright lights. But then they stopped, staring at where Jason's van should have been.

"He's gone," Sally said.

"Try call...," Andrew stopped in mid-sentence as two cars tore through the gates. "Mom!" He shouted, starting to run.

Mrs. Corbett's car squealed to a stop and she flung open her door, darting in front of the car behind her.

"Oh, Mom, Mom!...," Sally said, hurling herself into her mother's arms right behind Andrew. "We found them, we found them!"

"I know, darling, I know!" Mrs. Corbett's face was streaked with tears. "I was so frightened, so terrified, if anything had happened to you two I don't know what..." she started sobbing, unable to finish her sentence, squeezing them both so tightly they could hardly breathe.

Mr. Morrison's car had slid to a stop right behind Mom's and Henry ran too, surprised and pleased at how hard his dad's hug was. Finally his dad let go, and looked at his son. "How are you?"

At Henry's choked nod Mr. Morrison called loudly over the others' excited voices. "All right. Everyone stay here. I'm going inside to talk to the police."

He strode into the stable, coming quickly back with two officers. "These gentlemen will take your statements, and then, as our house is closest, I'd like to take you all there." He turned to Mrs. Corbett. "We can hear the whole story and get everyone fed and calmed down."

She nodded, still having trouble speaking, but Andrew said, "Great – I'm starving!"

Mrs. Morrison was waiting on their family's front steps to give Henry a huge hug. Then she turned to Mom. "I hope food will help," she said. "You must be in shock."

Mrs. Corbett nodded. "I think I am, but thank you. Thank you," she said, starting to cry again. "It's just that if anything had happened to my children, or your son…"

Sally felt her throat tighten and for a second tears welled in her eyes, but then she shook her head. "Mom, we are okay, and we got the toys back!"

Mr. Morrison cleared his throat. "Yes, you did. You did everything the police told you not to do, and you took some terrible chances," he said. "I hate to think what could have happened." He was trying to sound stern, but he couldn't hide how relieved he was. Then he shook his head, and they saw him smile. "And I'm very, very, proud of you."

"We can talk later about what might have happened," his wife interrupted. She put a bowl of salad on the kitchen table beside a big pot of crab gumbo and a basket of hot rolls.

"That looks wonderful." Mrs. Corbett smiled at Henry's mom. "I think I can finally eat, now that it's all over."

"But it's not over," Sally said, frowning. "Not until we know where Jason is."

Mr. Morrison helped himself to a roll. "You did say he wasn't hurt when he crashed his van, right?"

"It didn't seem like he was," Henry said. "He looked okay."

"We'll find him tomorrow, then, and I'll tell the Lt. how he helped you."

"But he did more than help us, he saved us." Sally's hair was flopping in her face, and she pushed it back with both hands. "And now he's not answering our texts or anything."

"I assure you I'll deal with it," Mr. Morrison said. "But there's nothing we can do tonight, and I'd still like to hear more about what happened."

Sitting in the spacious kitchen, refilling their plates and telling their stories made everyone feel better, until eventually Mrs. Corbett announced it was time for bed. She pointed at Fluffy, who had fallen asleep in the corner.

"She's got the right idea," she said, smiling.

But in the car Sally said, "Mom, I'm still worried about Jason."

Her mother looked at her in the rear view mirror. "I'm sure Mr. Morrison is right. He'll turn up tomorrow, and if he doesn't, the police will find him."

"But by then…" Sally began, and stopped when Andrew jabbed her in the ribs.

"Mom's right. He'll show up." Andrew sounded very sure. "Tomorrow."

"What's the matter with you?" Sally hissed. "You know Jason's not coming back. He's scared he's going to jail."

"Right," Andrew's voice was low. "So we've got to find him ourselves, before the police do. And make him come back on his own. That way he won't seem like a criminal."

Sally was quiet. Sometimes Andrew amazed her. "I thought you didn't like him," she said.

"That was then. This is now." Andrew made a face at her. "He saved us. I was really scared."

CHAPTER THIRTEEN

At the end of the dirt road Jason slowed the van, thinking. It didn't seem like the police were following him, but still he had to find a place to hide for the night. He knew his mom would be worrying, but he'd figure out a way to let her know he was okay, before he kept going tomorrow.

Ahead to the right he saw headlights speeding along a street. That would be Chamberlayne Avenue, which would take him north. He remembered there was a big park out this way — a perfect place to hide. He speeded up, which made his engine cough, but it seemed okay if he didn't go fast. Crashing into Ted's truck had not been the greatest idea he'd ever had, but he was still glad he'd done it. What, he wondered, would Ted have actually done if he hadn't come? Then he shook his head. He *had* gotten there, and all of them were safe. Even so, he'd never forgive himself for getting mixed up with Ted. How could he have been so stupid?

He knew it was better not to think about that, or about Sally and Andrew and Henry, so he concentrated on driving until he saw the park gate and swerved toward it. A rickety barrier saying 'Closed At Sunset' blocked the entrance, but he edged around it and in ten more minutes nosed the van into some shrubbery and cut the engine.

Then he just sat still. He listened to the hot engine thumping as it slowly cooled down, and then to the silence in the trees and playing fields around him. The stars were bright in the night sky and he heard an owl hooting, not far away. But in the silence, his worried thoughts came back. He wondered what was going on at the stable. And even more, what Sally and Andrew and Henry might be thinking.

"Don't be stupid," he said again. "They don't care about me, they probably didn't even notice I was gone."

But if he was honest, he knew that wasn't true. Sally did care. He could tell when they had that long talk on the sidewalk at Ted's house. She really liked that he wanted to be a history teacher. And he was pretty sure she'd care if he went to jail, which he definitely would if the police found him.

Andrew wasn't his biggest fan, but today they'd started to get along, and Henry had been okay the whole time – reserved, a bit quiet, but still okay.

But the professor...he couldn't stand remembering his being knocked unconscious. Now they'd never be able to finish their research together. *I'll probably get a police record too*, Jason thought, *and to make things worse, the police may have seen me holding a gun. At least I dropped it when they came inside.*

His phone beeped. Sally.

Where r u? Her text read. *Why did u take off like*

that? Can u please come back?

He sat up and stared at it, his feelings jumbled. Part of him wanted to turn around and go back right now, but another part, a bigger part, knew he couldn't. Maybe they do want me, he thought, but so do the police. There's no way I can go back. He shook his head, and looked at the text again. The more he read it, the worse he felt.

"I really like them," he said out loud. "It feels like I've known them my whole life, even though it's only been two days. I'd feel awful if I never saw them again."

A sad feeling came over him, and he turned off the phone and put it on the seat beside him. Then he leaned back and closed his eyes, and fell asleep.

"Wake up!" Andrew shouted, rushing into Sally's room. "It's him! He's in Bryan Park and he says he's okay!"

It was nearly eight o'clock, and sunbeams slanted across the floor as Sally sat up and squinted at Andrew's phone.

"We need to hurry," she said.

"Hold on," Andrew said. "I'll tell him we're coming, but we've got to figure out what to do when we get there."

"We're making Jason turn himself in. He has to," Sally said, jumping out of bed and looking for her bike shorts. She found them and hurried to the bathroom to splash water on her face.

"Right, but we haven't figured out how to make him," Andrew said. "He might just be telling us good bye."

"Well he can't," Sally said, drying her face. "We won't let him. And right now let's get downstairs. We have to act normal in front of Mom."

Mom and Jane and Mac were in the kitchen, and Mom gave them each a big hug. "I am so, so happy." She smiled at them as Mac handed them each a bowl of cereal.

"That's for sure." Mac grinned. "Great job, you two."

Jane had flung herself at Sally but Mom caught her by the arm. "You and Mac have to leave or you'll be late for school. You can hear everything later," she said.

"Have you called the Lt.?" Sally asked.

"The minute I get to my office. It doesn't help that Jason ran off like that, but Jim Morrison and I will do our best."

"He thought the police would arrest him," Andrew said. "His van's banged up, so he can't go very far. He's probably just trying to fix it."

"We'll see," Mom said. "And by the way, Mr. Morrison asked the police to collect your bikes, so they brought them back here early this morning. They're outside the side door. I'll be home for lunch. Maybe I'll have some news for you then."

She kissed them both, and they waited until the front door closed before Sally said, "Okay, call Henry. I wonder how much time we have before the police start looking."

"Not much," Andrew said, pulling out his phone. "And we still need to figure out what we're going to say to him."

"That he can't ruin his life," Sally said, guzzling some orange juice and grabbing leftover toast.

"We hope," Andrew said as he took his bike helmet off its hook and headed for the door.

Outside, Sally stood for a minute, looking at the sidewalks and grass plots, with sunlight pouring through the green branches and birds singing their usual songs. It seemed hard to believe everything that had happened yesterday. The world looked exactly the same, even though, for her, everything had changed. She smiled, jumped on her bike and followed Andrew, turning right on the Boulevard, toward Bryan Park.

Jason was standing just inside the park gates, giving a little wave as Henry rode up behind them. Jason pointed down the road to where they could all be out of sight behind a big beech tree.

"Hi," he said.

"Hi," they answered, suddenly not sure what to say, until Sally burst out.

"You were really dumb to run off like that," she said, surprised at how angry she felt. She propped her bike against the tree and tugged off her helmet.

"We've been thinking how to save you from the Lt.," Andrew said. He pulled up the front of his shirt to wipe his face.

"You can't save me from the Lt.," Jason said. "He wants to put me in jail, with Ted and Mike."

"Don't be so sure," Henry said. "The professor's on your side, and so are our parents. They're telling that to the police. But it'll only work if you go see the Lt. on your own, like you're not a criminal or anything."

Jason walked forward, his red hair gleaming in the sunlight. He looked rumpled and discouraged, and Sally felt sorry she'd yelled at him.

"You guys just don't get it," he said. "I did something illegal, and I can't change that. I have to leave."

Sally took a deep breath and made her voice quieter. "That's dumb too. You have to try. What about all the stuff we talked about, the professor, you being a teacher."

"That's gone," Jason said.

He started walking again, but Andrew blocked his way. "Nothing's gone. We got the toys back, which is huge. But you're the one who called the police. Our parents are telling them that too. So you need to go downtown, now."

Jason ran his hands through his hair, getting it back off his face. "You guys..." Abruptly he turned around as though he was going to leave, and Sally's heart sank. But then he turned back and faced them. "You guys..." he said again, "You're impossible. You need to forget about me and leave me alone."

"No way," Sally said. "We're not going to leave you

alone, and we're not going to forget about you, either."

No one moved while Jason looked at them for a minute more. Then, surprisingly, he smiled. "Okay. I'll go. But first I'm calling my mom. She worries."

They went over to their bikes, politely not listening while he walked a little way off, but they couldn't help hearing him say, "No, Mom, I'm doing this by myself. No, it'll be fine."

Then he came back, and Henry grinned at him. "We'll be around," he said.

"Okay," Jason said.

They watched his van disappear through the gates and then Sally turned to climb on her bike, the sun's glare making her squint. "Do you think they'll arrest him?"

Andrew looked at Henry. "Your dad's a lawyer. What do you think?"

"No way to know." Henry walked to his bike. "I hope not. But whatever happens, my Dad will help him. Right now, though, I've got to work."

"Me too," Andrew said. "But..." he hesitated, "Could you do us a favor?"

"Sure. What's up?"

"Can you come to our house with us later?"

"It'll keep Mom from getting mad," Sally added.

"Mad about what?" Henry looked puzzled.

"We sort of promised her we wouldn't look for Jason because the police were doing that," Andrew said. "She wanted us to stay out of it. It'd be a lot better if we all explain together, what we've just done."

"Ah, got it." Henry grinned. "How about we all stop work at noon, and I could come then."

"Great," Andrew said. "Meet us at Mr. Kelso's."

By the time Sally and Andrew pulled up to their first job the sun was pouring its heat onto the sidewalks. They could feel the concrete burning through their shoes, making it harder and harder to work as the morning wore on. Finally Andrew stopped, shoving his hair off his sweating face. "I can't understand why Jason hasn't texted us," he said. "It's close to twelve. I wonder if something bad's happened."

"He's never been great about texting," Sally said, turning off a hose.

"Yeah, but this is different. It's really important," Andrew said. "Anyway, it's gotten too hot to walk any more dogs, or cut grass. Let's go get Henry."

Henry was waiting in front of Mr. Kelso's house, and they pedaled slowly through the Fan District, staying in the shade of the big trees, thankful for any little breeze. Andrew was turning onto Monument Avenue when he stopped so suddenly Henry almost ran into him.

"Look." Andrew pointed at a TV truck and people with big cameras on their shoulders.

"They're in front of our house!" Sally said.

"Turn around, quick!" Andrew swung his bike sideways.

"The alley," Sally hissed.

They shot back to the side street and bumped as fast as they could down the alley's cobblestones to their back gate, quickly heaving their bikes into the garden.

"That was close," Andrew panted. The kitchen door was open, and they could see Mom inside.

"What's happened?" Sally called to her. "Why are those news people in front of our house?"

"Because you're famous," Mom called back, and they could see she was smiling. "They're trying to get in and talk to you."

Mac came out on the porch, and she was smiling too. "On the news they're calling you The Shockoe Slip Gang," she said.

"Wow," Andrew said. "What does that mean?"

"I don't know." Mom herded them inside and closed the door. "But the Lt. just called me."

Sally caught her breath, almost not wanting to know. "Jason?"

Mom nodded. "The police are looking for him, and they're wondering if you've heard from him."

For a minute they all stared at her, dumbfounded.

"But he texted this morning and said he was going to turn himself in..." Andrew stopped talking when he saw Sally's warning look. "You mean he's not at the police station?"

"Did my dad...?" Henry broke in.

"Yes," Mom said. "Your dad met with the Lt. this

morning and told him how Jason saved you three. The police will take that into account when they find him."

Seeing how upset they all looked, Mom sighed. "He might have planned to turn himself in, but maybe he decided to go and see his mother first, and had a change of heart. There's no way we can guess what he was thinking because people who're stressed often don't think very clearly. And right now, we have to eat lunch so we'll be on time for the press conference."

Sally's head turned. "Press conference?"

"Yes, at the museum this afternoon, at three. We're all going, you too," She said to Henry. "But meanwhile, welcome. I hope you'll stay for lunch."

No one talked very much while they ate. They were thinking about Jason, wondering if there was anything else they should have said. They were almost finished when, stuffed full of sandwiches and butterbeans, apple salad and ice cream, Sally looked around the table. "You know, I liked what that reporter called us. The Shockoe Slip Gang."

Andrew took a last spoonful of ice cream and wiped his mouth. "Yeah, it sounds like a movie, or a TV series."

"It would make a great name for our business," Sally went on, almost dreamily.

Andrew stared at her. "Are you talking about our yard business?"

Sally nodded. "I am." She looked at Henry. "We

could all be in it together, if you want to."

Henry grinned. "How could I not want to, with a name like that."

Andrew looked over at Jane. "You could work after school," he said, watching her face split into a huge smile.

"And," Sally went on, not sure where these ideas were coming from, but feeling good saying them, "we could have T-shirts with The Shockoe Slip Gang on them, like a regular business."

"Not bad," Andrew said. "Good, in fact. We'd be a company, a real company, with a name and everything." He gave a pleased sigh.

Mom had been listening, not saying a word, but now she pushed her chair back from the table. "I think this is a wonderful idea, for all of you. It's a great plan." She stood up. "But we need to get to the museum very soon, or we'll be late." She chuckled. "And that would not be good."

"Ready for this, everyone?" Henry's dad said in a cheerful voice. They were all standing just outside the Museum's main hall, looking through a curtain at the heavy camera rigs and floodlights that were set up all around the big room, which was filled with people.

"We are," the professor said, while Henry and Andrew stared nervously through the curtain at the mob of reporters.

A week ago this same room had had a sad feeling, almost an air of gloom, Sally thought. But now she could almost feel a sense of joy, seeing it in people's faces and their smiles and hearing it in their voices, as though the museum was humming with happiness. She could see Jane at the side of the room, standing with Mac and jumping up and down with excitement. Sally wanted to wave at them, realizing she was beginning to feel excited too.

"This is really fun!" she whispered to Henry.

"It's pretty cool," he whispered back, watching the camera crews barking orders at the men rolling wires across the floor while the TV anchors fiddled with their microphones and the reporters pulled out their pencils.

But suddenly, without any warning, Sally thought of Dad. A bolt of pain shot through her stomach, and she wanted to see him and talk to him so desperately she felt dizzy. We did this for you, Dad, she whispered, and the family, and you don't even know. She put up her fist and clenched her jaw to stop the sobs that were starting in the middle of her chest. She knew they could take over her whole body, right here in front of everyone, and she drew in a long, shuddering breath.

"You okay?" Henry was looking at her.

She nodded. "I wish my Dad was here," she said in a wobbly voice.

"He is," Henry said, "I mean, in your head. From

what my Dad told me about him, you're lucky you had a father like that. He'd be really proud of you."

Stunned, Sally looked down at the floor. "Thank you..." she managed to say, as a TV assistant rushed through the curtain, herding everyone toward the podium.

"More later," Henry whispered.

The big room grew quiet, and Mr. Morrison stepped forward. "This is indeed a marvelous day for our museum," he began. "Only one week ago many of you gathered here to learn some very bad news – our museum had been robbed. A number of antique toys, collected for an exhibit scheduled to open this Fall, were stolen by professional thieves who were prepared to sell them on the black market. But today you'll hear wonderful news. We have recovered every single one of the toys. The crowd began to applaud and he had to stop. "Thanks to three very brave and resourceful young people, who are standing with me this afternoon."

He pushed them forward to wave as all the reporters, TV anchors, and onlookers began to cheer and clap.

"The Shockoe Slip kids!" Someone called out, and someone else called, "How does it feel to be heroes?"

"We're not heroes," Henry said.

"That's what the police Lt. called you," the first voice said.

"We just wanted to get the toys back. And help our mom," Andrew said, feeling secretly pleased.

"Were you scared when that guy, Ted, came in the barn?" Another reporter had her notebook open and was scribbling in it. "And what's this about knocking him down with a horse?"

"We were scared," Sally said, relieved her voice was steady again. "But mostly we were really mad."

"Sounds like you really were a gang – a pretty determined gang of kids, facing some very determined thieves," the reporter said, still scribbling.

"I'm not sure we were a gang then," Andrew began. "But we're a gang now. We've started a new lawn and pet care business, and that's our company's name. The Shockoe Slip Gang."

The reporter looked up and smiled as Mom stepped forward and grabbed Andrew's arm. "Well, I wish you luck, and a lot of customers."

"Mom!" Andrew protested in a low voice, "I just want to tell people about our website."

"What do you mean?" Sally hissed. "We haven't got a website!"

"True, but we're definitely getting one," he whispered back. "We'll be swamped with new clients after this."

Now the reporters' questions came even faster, and everyone took turns answering until finally Mr. Morrison stepped forward.

"I have more news." He held up his hand to quiet the applause. "We've made an equally wonderful and totally unexpected discovery this morning – an original letter, written by Alexander Hamilton to General Washington's aide, the Marquis de Lafayette. It was found by Dr. Montague Saunders" – he gestured sideways at the professor – "inside one of the toys, a wooden pull toy owned by a family in Philadelphia."

A sudden, startled silence fell over the room and then the applause became a roar as reporters, TV anchors, crew and onlookers crowded around the podium until the senior anchorman shouted above the din, "Quiet! Quiet!"

"I'll let Professor Saunders explain," Mr. Morrison said.

The professor stepped to the microphone, smiling. "I don't think the museum expected us to find anything," he said. "In fact, I'm not sure anyone did. But for many years I've had a theory, and today that theory has proved to be true."

When the professor finished speaking and the questions ended, Mr. Morrison led them back through the curtain and pulled it closed. "We can watch ourselves on the news tonight." He smiled. "I'm proud of every single one of you."

The professor was smiling as well, looking at Sally and Andrew and Henry. "And if you three get here early tomorrow morning, I can give you a special peek at the letter."

"We'd really like that," Henry said.

"Yes, thank you," Sally said, and then, seeing the expression on the professor's face, she took a chance.

"You haven't heard from Jason either?"

"No." His smile faded. "All very unfortunate. We can only hope this will get resolved somehow."

"They'll love seeing the letter." Mom broke in. "It's a wonderful discovery. But right now it's time to go home."

At the house Mom came over and put her arms around Sally and Andrew. "Let's sit down," she said.

She led them to the living room sofa, her face serious. "You two may have to accept that Jason isn't coming back," she said gently. "And you may never know why."

For a minute Andrew and Sally just stared at her. "But I think we sort of do know why." Sally broke the silence. "He kept saying he committed a crime, and it would be on his record forever. He kept saying he was just a scholarship kid that no one cared about except the professor. So he doesn't think he can ever get to be a history teacher."

"He was probably lying," Andrew said bitterly. "All that other stuff he talked about, like helping the professor find the letters. That was probably a lie too. He really let us down."

Mom leaned back against the pillows. "Well, he's certainly hurt you," she said. "Being disappointed by someone feels terrible, especially if it's someone you liked a lot. But he wouldn't have taken you to Ted's house, and later crashed his van at the stable, if he didn't care about the letters, and about you. Maybe you should try to remember the good things about him."

Andrew sat up and stretched. "Maybe," he said. "I'll think about it." Then he looked at Sally. "We still need to walk a couple of dogs and feed some cats, but if we hurry we can get back in time to watch us on the news."

"Right." She reached over and gave Mom a hug. "And see our famous mother on TV."

Andrew grinned. "And hear what I said about the almost famous Shockoe Slip Lawn and Pet Care company."

EPILOGUE

After supper, Sally and Andrew kicked off their shoes and went out in the yard. Jane brought Peaches, and they flopped down on their backs in the dew-soaked grass, letting its wetness cool them. Grass had a different smell when it was damp, Sally thought. More alive, somehow, like being on a farm and smelling big fields. Peaches lay on Jane's stomach, purring loudly, and Jane pulled off her glasses.

"Do you think the professor'll find any more messages in the toys?" She said.

Andrew rolled over on his side. "Probably," he said. "Except I've been wondering about that. I mean, I still don't get why those guys like George Washington would send messages in a bunch of wooden toys. I know it was secret, but what was wrong with just writing letters in code? That would've been a lot easier."

"People can figure codes out," Sally said. "If the British did and got hold of a letter, they'd know what George Washington was planning. Like crossing the Delaware or something. No one would think of looking in a kid's toy."

Andrew yawned. "What's really weird is how slow everything was," he said. "They didn't even have phones

or cars, so they couldn't get messages fast. All they could do was ride horses."

Sally thought that would have been wonderful, but she stopped talking as they all lay still, watching the moon rise. It was huge and mysterious, and they could feel the garden around them throbbing with life – every kind of bug humming, buzzing, or zinging away with its own music, and occasional squalls from cats in the alley adding to the pulsing sounds of a July night. All of a sudden Sally felt a surge of happiness. The summer wasn't even half over, and there was still plenty of time to do all kinds of stuff. They could work in their new company and make money, she could practice her running, maybe even start training for one of the races Henry went to. Maybe the police would let her go back and see Chief too, and in August they might go to their cousin's farm in Smithfield and camp out. Even though it had only been a few days, it seemed a long time ago when she'd been lying on this garden's wall, wanting Zorro and his gang to gallop their horses right up to their house and help them. Now she only felt pleased she'd learned she hadn't really needed any help.

"Well, maybe we did need Jason's van," she said aloud.

"What?" Andrew mashed a mosquito on his arm.

"Unimportant." She lifted Peaches off Jane's stomach and sat up. "They're starting to bite, we'd better go inside."

But as they trailed across the grass she stopped. "Remember that day I told you nothing exciting ever happens in Richmond?" She said.

"I do," Andrew grinned. "But it did."

Jane started doing a little dance around them. "So what can you make happen next?" She crooned.

"Something fun," Andrew said, poking her in the stomach.

"Something exciting," Sally said, and even though he couldn't see Sally's face in the dark, Andrew knew she was smiling.

THE END

THE AUTHOR

Patricia Cecil Hass grew up in Richmond, Virginia, riding her bicycle, raising dogs, and racing homing pigeons. She has been a journalist, an editor and is the author of three earlier mid-grade mysteries. She lives in Princeton, New Jersey.

THE ILLUSTRATOR

Laura Corson lives in Richmond, Virginia, and enjoys using graphite, pen and ink, watercolor, colored pencils, and digital art programs to create her work. She is inspired by childhood cartoons, lifelike realism, and fantasy art.

CPSIA information can be obtained
at www.ICGtesting.com
Printed in the USA
BVHW041141101121
621056BV00026B/499/J